THE
CARVING
PLACE

THE CARVING PLACE

Publishing Copyright ©2018 Laurel Rose Publishing

Laurel Rose Publishing
www.laurelrosepublishing.com
laurelrosepublishing@gmail.com

Cover art and graphics by Tammy Gallina

ISBN: 978-1-944583-21-7

Dedication
Hayley Cathey Dandridge

While the character of Asa Sinclair resembles my father in his manner and sayings, nothing of his life story compares to that of my father or any member of our family. The setting of Sinclair Farm is inspired by family farmland in Tate County, Mississippi. Nothing remains today of the house, outbuildings, livestock, or other elements mentioned in this book, except the corncrib.

ANCESTORS

Up from the land the ancestors call
Remember us they say
Remember our toils and our trials
Carry us with you day by day
Seek to find the old pathways
Remember the old landmarks
Never forget from whence you've come
As on life's journeys you do embark
Cherish our stories and lessons
Hold them ever dear
In all of your remembrances
We are kept forever near
—*Patricia Neely-Dorsey, 2014*

Part I, Mississippi
Chapter 1
Lora • 1982 • Mississippi

I am sitting in the hundred-year old corn crib on my grandparent's farm in North Mississippi. Actually, I'm perched on the rough log window on the side of the crib. There are rodents and maybe snakes down in that corn, I'm sure. I've heard rustling and scampering down in the corn when I opened the half door used to get to the corn.

So I'll just stay up here in the window.

The side window of the crib looks out on one of the horse pastures. This is my favorite spot. If I'm brave enough, I can get an ear or two of corn and call the horses, and they will come from the backside of the pasture.

"Never lie to your horses," my granddaddy says. "If you rattle a bucket or call them with feed, you better give them some. It won't be long before they quit believing you."

Daddy can take an ear of that hard, yellow horse corn and wring it in his big hands, and corn will fall right into the bucket. Buck can do it, too. I can't. My hands are too small. Maybe if I'm lucky, I can pick off a few kernels.

When the horses come up for their treat, I can throw the corn in the old molasses tub on the ground, and if I stretch my skinny legs as far as they can go, I can run my bare feet through their manes as they eat. There is nothing like that feeling.

Then I watch them as they drink from an old galvanized tub, the muscles in their sleek necks pushing the water down their throats in a rush. There is a worn path leading from the pasture to that spot by the corn crib. They have travelled that path many times over the years at feeding time. The shade of the crib and the gnarled limbs on the ancient oak tree make it a favorite shady spot in the late afternoon.

After eating, the small herd stands with their heads level with their backs, eyes closed, tails gently swishing away pesky flies, and doze in the afternoon heat.

Daddy says I'm not supposed to go barefooted around the horses. I could step on a nail and get tetanus. Then I'd have to get shots in my stomach, I've heard. So before I go back to the house, I better put my shoes back on.

When I'm sitting in that window, I pretend that I'm in Africa on safari and that those are wild horses, sometimes zebras. Or I can be a wild child who lives deep in the forest with no one for company but animals. Come to think of it, that's kinda true.

Daddy also says that I'm not supposed to talk baby talk to the horses and pet them on their faces. "They will forget they are horses and start thinking they are people," he says. I try to go by all his rules, but I break this one when he is not around. In fact, when he didn't think I was looking, I've even seen him run his hand down the face of his horse after a good ride.

I guess he just doesn't want us to have any biting horses. So far, so good.

I think I'm the luckiest kid in the South to live on this farm. There isn't anything fancy about the old farmhouse, built 150 years ago. But it holds our family history and a little mystery to boot.

I live here on this farm with my Daddy, Granddaddy, Grandmother, Buckshot, and Aunt Shelly.

After Mama died, Shelly came to live with us to take care of me. Mama died when I was real little. I just barely remember her. If I shut my eyes real hard, I think I can feel her hand on my head, smoothing my hair when I had a fever. I'm probably remembering Grandmamma Lydia.

Mama and Daddy had only been married three years when she died. I do just fine here with my assorted family.

I think aunts may be better than mothers sometimes. Shelly is younger than my mother was. I get to go to her room at night and listen to the latest, cool music on her stereo. Granddaddy doesn't think too much of her music. She fixes my hair, 'cause when Daddy does it, it looks pretty bad. It's real thick and hangs in my eyes like the forelock on one of the horses.

She knows how to braid it and get it under control.

Shelly grew up in Memphis. She wasn't a farm girl like me—doesn't love horses and dogs like I do. Well, she likes them okay, but likes city stuff and music more.

The house was originally a dog trot house. This means that there were two original rooms with an open porch in the middle. Down here it gets so hot. I can't imagine no air conditioning. I can just see my great-grandparents sitting in that hall, shelling peas or butterbeans with a dog at their feet.

Long before I was born, the hall was enclosed and a kitchen, dining room, some small bedrooms and bathroom were added, so I don't remember the dogtrot.

Now Grandmama works on her peas in the kitchen, washing them in a big, white, enamel farm sink. She sits on a short chair and shells them over a bucket while she watches her soap operas on a little TV in the kitchen.

You might call Grandmama Lydia a country type grandma. I can tell she was really pretty when she was young. Now she wears her hair up most of the time, with little silver sprigs always escaping around her face when she is hot. And that's most of the time. She works in the garden, feeds animals, cooks for all of us. She doesn't have time for curlers or make-up. But when she does dress up for church or some other dressy occasion, she makes me smile.

I love listening to Grandmama and her friends talk—about the weather, their men, the crops, what they need, and what they'd have if they could. But more than what they talk about, I like to listen to the voices. I sit on my little stool in the corner, pretending to be reading, and listen. You learn a lot like that.

They look like old ladies to me, with their work dresses on, hair pulled back or put up. But after you listen to them for a while and hear them talk about what they did when they were young, they don't seem so old at all.

These are all Southern women, born and raised. Yet their accents are different. My Grandmama Lydia has what I guess is a gentle Southern accent. She drops her "R's," like cella' instead of cellar, coner instead of corner. On the other hand, her friend Sadie adds "R's to the ends of words—like winder instead of window.

Cudin' Ida has the most lyrical speaking voice to me. I don't know how to describe it. She never uses words wrong and sounds like one of the stars in the old movies, kind of like people from England sound. I listened to Katharine Hepburn or Rita Hayworth. They drop their "R's" too but sound like rich folks.

I know how they sound 'cause Shelly lets me come to her room late at night and watch old movies on her little TV that sits in the window with its rabbit ears wrapped in foil to catch the best signal.

The two original rooms are now big bedrooms. My grandparents' room is so big it's used for sleeping, and there are rocking chairs and a sittin' area around a gas heater where there was once a fireplace. The ceilings in there are real tall, maybe 10 feet high. I love it when it is cold and I come in the house. That gas heat has a smell all its own, and to me, it smells like home in the winter.

My bedroom is one of the added-on rooms at the back of the house. Mine has a big iron bed, painted white, and a grandmother's flower garden quilt that I found in the attic.

Buck has the other added on room, which is smaller than mine, and Shelly has the bedroom that Grandmama Lydia used to call her sewing room. Shelly hung up a curtain to separate her part of the room and Grandmama's sewing machine and material.

The other big bedroom has been used by different people over time. It was my parent's room and now my Daddy's. It has a real fireplace and the ceilings are low since the attic part is overhead.

Behind a door, that looks like a closet, are stairs that go to the attic—also one of my favorite places to sit, go through old stuff, and pretend.

Sometimes I go up in the attic and pretend that I am Anne Frank, hiding from the Nazis. There is a small boarded off room up there. I wonder if someone lived up there at one time. Now it's just a kind of closet. That space is a little creepy, like maybe someone was locked in there.

But most of my pretend time in the attic is good. Instead of making that closet a creepy place, maybe it's kind of like the wardrobe in The Chronicles of Narnia that leads to an enchanted place. Or it might be a good place to hide from the Yankees if you lived during the Civil War times.

The fourth step to the attic has a secret compartment. The top comes up. You'd never know it was there. I like to think that in the old days the family kept treasures or old pistols in that space, but I don't really know what all was kept in there.

My friends who come to visit me say when you come down the gravel drive to our house, it's like going back in time about thirty years. We do live a little different out here. Maybe it's the old house. We have modern things too, but there is just an overall feeling that you are in a different world and time.

Buck is about two years older than I am. He and his mother used to live on our place in a small wood frame house. Paulette was kind of attractive in an ordinary way. They grew peas, corn, butterbeans, and she had a really amazing flower garden. Ladies in town used to come out and cut fresh flowers there when they were having company or when someone died. Sometimes Paulette worked in town for a local florist, but I don't think they paid her right.

She had a way of putting a few flowers in an old enamel pitcher, or a tin bucket, and they looked better than if you'd gotten them in town. Paulette used wildflowers and a few special flowers she grew behind the little house like Queen Anne's Lace, Aster, and Foxglove. To make the arrangement have a look that you wouldn't find in town, she would get curly willow or just some ordinary greenery to drape over the container. I don't really remember this, but Shelly has told me.

When Buck was about five years old, she drove up to our house and told Daddy that she couldn't stand the hard work anymore and was leaving to go live with her brother in Tennessee. She left Buck there on the porch with his few things in two brown grocery sacks. So Buck lives with us in the other added-on room.

He must have missed his Mama, but he never cried for her, that I know of. It's kind of like having a brother, but not really. He has a real name, something ordinary like John or Jim, but Daddy started calling him Buckshot, and it stuck. We just shorten it to Buck most of the time.

Buck is a good looking boy, all my friends say, with his blonde hair that always needs cutting and his blue-gray eyes. He can do any chore Daddy gives him, but I don't think he does good in school. He isn't bad, and never has to stay after school, but he really has trouble reading. Sometimes I read him his homework, even though I'm younger, and it seems to help him learn better. It is always bad around here when he brings home his report card. Bad news. Daddy just shakes his head.

Chapter 2
Buckshot • 1982 • Mississippi

My name is John Toliver, but around here I go by Buckshot or Buck for short. I don't know what I'd have done if Mr. Asa hadn't taken me in when Mama left. She just got tired of all that digging in the dirt, sweatin', pickin' peas, shellin' peas, pickin' butterbeans, shellin' butterbeans.

Those women in town liked her flowers better than the ones in a flower shop. Mama had an eye for making them look special in vases or pitchers. She barely had enough money for us to get by. But somehow we always managed.

Mr. Asa has been payin' me since I was eight years old to help him, and I'm 14 now. Mostly I ride in the truck with him to do whatever he's doing.

"Hey there Buckshot," he says. "Climb up in here and let's go to work."

I like checking cows the best. He counts each cow, calf, and bull, using his own system in his head. He calls out the numbers to me and tells me to write them down in a little black journal that he got at the feed store. Sometimes I get the numbers backward. He can tell when I do that, but never yells at me.

Every now and then, he will give me his little cow countin' clicker, a small stainless steel piece that is about as big as a walnut. It has a little clicker on top. You click for every cow, and a number shows up on a dial. I start out doing real good til' the cows move around and then I get mixed up. Most of them are black and white face cows with a few Hereford cross. Anyway, I write my numbers next to his, and we take a look at them.

Mr. Asa speaks in a low, soft voice. Hardly

ever yells at anything—me, the cow dogs, the horses, or Lora. But sometimes she makes him shake his head, and that makes me laugh inside.

Another thing we do is fix fences. I don't like doing that too much. Mr. Asa pulls the bob wire tight with a contraption called a fence stretcher. Seems like we are always fencing when it is the hottest day of the summer or the coldest day of winter.

I stand beside him with a bag of staples and hand him one when he asks for it. Sometimes I get to day dreaming, and he has to thump on the bill of my cap to get my attention. I like that bag, though. It's made out of the top of an old beat up, tan, cowboy boot with fancy leather toolin' on it. He fixed a looped strap sewn on top so I can hook it over a saddle horn or my shoulder if we are on foot.

My best day is when he says, "Buck, go saddle us a couple of horses." I run to the pasture and get our two best cow horses. We could get up cows like most people do, in the truck, but we like to do things "the cowboy way." Mr. Asa and I saddle up and ride at a nice walk down to the pasture to check the fences and the cows, too. We just walk real quiet-like around the cows and up and down the fence rows. Mr. Asa is looking for places to spray the weeds around the fence posts, and I'm looking for holes and hoping we don't find any.

When we work on fences he can tell I'm gettin' tired and red in the face. Then we go over to a shady spot, put down the tailgate of his truck, and he opens an old fishin' cooler that has grape sodas or Cokes in it. He opens an old lunch box, and it has 'minter cheese sandwiches wrapped in wax paper that Miss Shelly or Mrs. Lydia made early that morning. There might be chocolate cake or cookies that they call tea cakes in there, too. Tea cakes just don't make sense to me. Sounds too fancy. They are just big, chewy cookies, my favorite.

Today we are cleanin' up around the little house mama and I used to live in. It's in pretty fair shape, but it's growed up bad and needs painting. I think maybe another family may need to move in there for a while. So I'm pulling weeds. I can see in the windows where the same red and white checked curtains mama made are still hanging on the rods.

She's been gone for a while now. Every few

months she sends me little letters with a few dollars in the envelopes. All I know is that she is still living with her brother and working at a truck stop in Tennessee. I don't blame her for leaving'. It was a hard life for her, and she could do better.

Pullin' up rotten boards on the porch, I see on the bare dirt and dug out places that dogs have made to keep themselves cool. We did have a little dog when I lived here. He was brown and white and jumped a lot. Maybe he dug those holes. Maybe it was something wild.

Chapter 3
Lora • 1982 • Mississippi

When I got up this morning, Daddy told me he was taking me with him horseback to check fences. I loved to ride out on the place with him. He looks like the perfect cowboy when he is on a horse. He doesn't wear any of that fancy cowboy attire just a plaid shirt, well-worn jeans, his working boots and his hat, set at just the right angle on his head.

Daddy is a handsome man in my book. He is tall for his generation, about 6-2. His years in the sun have brought creases around his eyes and on his forehead. Even though he's not that old, his thick, brown hair is beginning to get a little gray around the temples. He keeps it cut close to his head these days.

I guess maybe I got my hair from him and my eyes from my mother, from pictures I've seen. Hope I don't start getting gray soon. Since I'm just 12, maybe that won't be for a while.

I can tell when Daddy is getting tired by the way he sits in the saddle. I know some days he has worked hard all day but finds time to spend a little time with me riding. Those days he slumps a little in the saddle. He is just riding, not like he would if he was working on a new horse. Then he sits straight, makes contact with the horse's mouth, and uses his legs. I never will learn all that secret horse language. I'm lucky he lets me ride a good-broke horse that takes care of me.

Most of the time when we ride, we just talk. I like that. Sometimes he sees me do something wrong and shows me the right way to do it. But it's not like he's fussin'.

"Heels down, toes up, Lori-girl. You're riding on the tips of your toes."

"Put your hand down and stay out of his mouth. If you stay in his mouth all the time, he won't respond when you really need to get his attention. Keep your hands quiet."

After riding fences for what seemed like a long time, we go by another one of my favorite places besides the corncrib window, our carving tree. It is a big old American Beech tree about 150 years old. It stands tall in the woods behind our house on the way to the cow pasture. As we approached the tree he stopped and got off his horse.

"Get down from there Lori-girl. We've got some business to take care of." I got off my horse and walked over to where he was standing. I didn't see anything at first. Following his glance, I noticed the names and writing on the trunk of the big tree. It was so big around that if Daddy and I held hands, we still couldn't reach around it.

"Old folks used Beech trees for carving because their bark is smooth," he said, kneeling down and wiping his ever-present pocket knife on the knee of his jeans. I'd seen him use that same pocket knife to cut leather, trim a rough spot on a horse's hoof, and even cut into a watermelon. It had about five blades. "It's time we added your name."

He showed me where he and my mother had carved their initials not long after they got married. His were bold and strong—AVS. I could see my grandmother Lydia's name along with other family initials. It was getting harder to read some of them. The initials did not grow up with the tallness of the tree but got bigger around. Carvings much older than Daddy's were beginning to stretch and blur.

I ran my fingers across the marks—another reminder that my mama had really been here, on this farm, at this spot, loving Daddy. That made me happy.

Daddy had let Buck carve on the tree last summer. Instead of his initials for John Toliver, he had just written "Buck." I could tell that his carving was much newer than the rest—clean and sharp. There were some random initials of people we didn't know. Daddy said they were probably friends of our family, or maybe of a hunter who just found the tree in the woods.

While I watched, Daddy outlined the initials of my name, Lora Madison Sinclair.

Then he gave me the knife and let me chip at the inside of the letters, making them deeper. I chipped and chipped until my hand hurt. He took the knife and finished carving LMS and the date. The oldest carving I could still read was 1920-something.

"Why do we do this?" I asked, squinting up at him. He smiled down and said, "Just to prove we were here—at this place, on our land. It's where we belong. Let's mount up, Lori-girl."

And off we went, over a little creek. He always stopped in the creek with the cool water running across his horse's feet, put his hand down on his horse's neck, relaxing the reins, and let his horse drink. "That way, he won't dread going across the water," he said.

He nodded for me to do the same. We let the horses pull in the clear, cold water until they raised their heads, water dripping from their mouths. "Let's go before they start pawing," he winked. "That signals they are about to roll. Have to beat them to it."

And with just a cluck, he and his horse were climbing out of the creek and up the bank. I looked back at the name tree. That was a good day.

After riding all afternoon, I put up my horse up like I'm supposed to. He was hot, so I just washed off his feet and brushed him out good—mane and tail, and turned him out to graze. I could tell I smelled like horse sweat, so I sat down on the steps of the front porch.

I hope I remember this porch 'til the day I die. The porch runs across the front of the house. There are two white wood swings, facing each other. I got to swinging too high one time when I was little, and the swing flipped and dumped me like a buckin' horse. Sometimes we eat watermelon out on the porch on Sunday after church. We keep a horse or two in the yard sometimes. It's not a yard like those at the country club in town. Grandmamma Lydia has a flower bed, but it is behind a little iron fence to keep the horses, or whatever we have in there, from getting her flowers and shrubs.

So the air at night has a slight musty horse smell mixed with the scent of her flowers. Sometime you get a whiff of honeysuckle. If

Asa sees it creeping around on his fences, he gets out his spray rig, and goodbye honeysuckle.

The side porch is what my grandmother calls the sleeping porch. She said when she was my age, and there was no air conditioning, she and her mother used to sleep out there in the summer months, like July and August, when it is really hot in Mississippi. Asa did too.

The porch is still furnished like that, with two iron frame twin beds. The frames don't match exactly, but they are both painted white, now a chipped white. There are bed linens on them in the summer, old quilts and old bedspreads. Daddy gets me to take them in for the winter. We also have a rocking chair or two and a porch table. Grandmamma has a few plants sitting around on the porch. Some are philodendrons and petunias that are getting kinda' leggy. We stay so busy with regular farm chores that we forget about the porch plants.

Daddy and I sit out there sometimes in the fall, and in the mornings he takes his coffee out there and rocks. Buck still sleeps out there in the summer every once in a while. He says he likes to go to sleep listening to the frogs and crickets. He loves the night sounds. When he comes in the house in the mornings, his hair is sticking up all over his head from the morning dew and dampness.

I used to wonder what my friends would think of me, living out here in the country like folks did 50 years ago. It's funny. They like to come here and see the horses and dogs more than they want me to come to town to hang out with them or go shopping at the mall. Don't know if they like the horses, the sleeping porch or Buck.

One time two of my friends from town came to spend the night and they wanted to sleep on the porch. Well, that didn't last long. As soon as it got dark, the humid air settled on the bed covers, making them feel damp. We saw a few lightening bugs, and they liked that. But when the sun finally went down and it got country dark, the crickets started chirping real loud.

Not long after that, I heard an owl. I looked over and Cindy was sitting up in her bed looking bug-eyed. "Lora, what is THAT?"

"Oh just a little owl," I said. It was not a big deal in my book.

"Can we have a light out here," asked Sara, with a quiver in her voice.

"No. Then we can't see the lightening bugs and the moon and stars. It would ruin everything." I must have come off like a know-it-all country girl, and they didn't like that.

"Oh, please get a flashlight," pleaded Sara.

I went in the kitchen and came back with a big work flashlight. I thought this might calm them down. I shone it around on the floor of the porch, on their beds, under the beds, out the sides of the porch.

When I shone it on the door of the porch, there perched for us to see was a cute little tree frog. He was light green and stretched out in all his glory on the door. Helping him hang on were his four long orange toes with the little suction cups on the end.

The girls squealed and jumped in their beds and covered their heads. I told them he couldn't get in the door.

Just as we started to settle down again, I heard a screaming out in the woods behind one of the barns. And then the cow dogs started barking and making a fuss.

"And, WHAT is THAT?" asked Sara. "The

dogs must think there is something out there."

"That's a female fox call. It's called the vixen scream. She's just looking for a mate. I hope she's not too close to the chickens." I thought to myself, I better tell Asa about that in the morning.

We tried again for sleep. I had just gone to sleep when I woke up to see Cindy standing next to my bed, looking me straight in the eye. "Lora, I want to go home."

Cindy had long, dark hair with just enough curl in it that the night air was making it curl and wave all around her head. With her wild hair, sprinkling of freckles across her nose, and big wide-open green eyes, she was quite a sight.

So we went in the house and went to the old black phone in the hall. We didn't have phones all over the house like my city friends did.

Cindy called her mama, which I'm sure didn't go over well. I could tell by her end of the conversation that her mama was telling her to be a big girl and to tough it out til morning.

I heard Cindy start crying and telling her about the screaming in the woods that sounded like a woman being murdered. Her mama had to come five miles out here in the dark to get her.

When Cindy's mama got here, I looked over at Sara. Her bag was packed too. "Since y'all are going to town, can I have a ride?"

I rolled my eyes. After they left, I went to my bedroom inside. I'd have to clean up the porch in the morning and explain to everyone where my friends were. With all that coming and going, Asa, Buck, Shelley, and Grandmama Lydia never woke up. When you work hard, you sleep hard.

Part II
"Almost Heaven, West Virginia"
Chapter 4
Lora • 1997 • West Virginia

The air smells different here in West Virginia, clean and clear, but with an aroma of times past—wood smoke, evergreens, a sweet musky smell. A cooler kind of moisture hangs in the air. If you looked hard you could see big webs the spiders had woven between the pines, just waiting for someone to walk right into them.

After college at The University of Mississippi where I got a Bachelor's degree in Southern Studies, I had a hard time finding myself. I distanced myself from all that was familiar.

My grandparents died within two years of each other about the time I finished college. Even though I had a wonderful but sheltered childhood on the farm, I wanted to see what else there was out there. After managing a small art gallery in St. Louis, I wrote some grants for historical projects, had a bad relationship or two, and found myself in limbo.

I found a short-term project that sent me here to study the culture of the mountain people and compare it to the culture of the South. Right up my alley. After clearing it with Asa, I packed and left for Appalachia.

Asa's health is declining, but he insisted he'd be fine with Buck to help and Sadie to come around when he needs her. The last time I saw him, I could tell the creases around his eyes had deepened, and he didn't stand as straight as he always had.

He was glad for me to go and said that he would have jumped at the chance to see more of the world when he was my age. I promised myself after about six weeks on the job, I'd fly home to check on him, and Buck, and the farm.

After my flight, I finally found a taxi that

would take me to start my journey into Appalachia, beginning with a small rural community in the foothills of the mountains. My college roommate had given me the name of a friend up here, and it was time for me to give him a call.

The taxi ride cost a fortune, but I had expected that. I stood there with my two bags and a satchel that I would use to hold my research notes. My camera was in my purse.

I found myself at a little country store that seemed to be quite a hub of activity for this small community. Two mixed-breed hound dogs lay on the porch, thumping their tails on the wood planks but never raising their heads as I climbed the old wooden steps to the porch.

I went in the store, looking for a pay phone. "What do you need?" asked the woman working behind the counter. She was a small woman who wore a faded blue smock and had old, scuffed leather sandals on her feet. She had dark brown eyes that twinkled from behind deep wrinkles in her browned skin. Her brown hair had sprinkles of gray around her temples, and was worn in a ponytail, low on her head, and down her back.

'I'm Jolie," she told me. At first glance I thought she might be in her seventies but soon realized that she was much younger. Mountain life is hard.

"Do you have a pay phone," I asked.

"No, but if the call is local, you can use the phone there on the counter."

I called my contact and sat down in a twisted willow-back chair to wait for him to come.

"You ain't from around here, are you?"

"No, ma'am. I'm from Mississippi. I'm waiting on someone. Do you mind if I sit here until he comes?" She just smiled.

It was pretty clear that there wasn't going to be a big store anywhere around, so I looked around while I waited to see if I needed any supplies. There were glass jars with red tops holding big lemon cookies. I hadn't seen them since I was about ten.

Finally, I went to the counter and asked Mrs. Jolie for a Coke. "A pop? Sure, what kind?" she said.

"A Coke." I took my seat in an old rocker and drank my Coke from a clear green bottle while I looked out the window.

I made a mental note that she might be a

good source when I started my research. She didn't say anything but reached into one of the glass jars and handed me a lemon cookie.

I noticed two older men in overalls who had been sitting by a wood stove looking over at me. No stove was needed in the early fall, but that seemed to be their talking and rocking spot. I guess there are pockets of older men sitting around stoves, at tables and booths all across the country. In our little town in Mississippi, you will find several different groups at restaurants, coffee shops, gas stations, and country stores. They meet, sit, rock, and solve the world's problems.

A younger man about my age appeared from the back of the store. He strode through, taking long, bouncy steps. "Hey, are you waiting for someone?"

"A guy named Sam Wood is supposed to meet me here," I said looking up. "Do you know him?" He was about medium height, and had his long straight hair pulled back in a short ponytail. His beard was neatly trimmed.

"Sam?" he said with amusement. "Knowing him is an understatement." He nodded to the store window. "I'm Rex."

I looked up to see a cloud of dust as an old brown pickup pulled up in front of the store. When the dust cleared, I saw a tall, thin, lanky man, striding toward me. His long legs were clad in old jeans that were worn at the back, dragging in the dirt at his boot heel. He wore a brown shirt with the sleeves rolled up and an Australian outback hat. The dark brown hair curled from underneath his hat and rested on the collar of his shirt.

"I'm Sam Wood, you must be Lora." I stood and shook his hand. He nodded at the other guy, and they both broke out in broad smiles. "See you, Rex."

"Well, you wanna' get in the truck and let me see if I can figure out a place for you to stay?" He took my things around to his side of the truck and threw them in. Looking back at the store, I received a shock as I stood there by the truck door. A big, wet tongue licked the whole side of my face. I turned in time to back up and see a big, black lab just laughing at me.

"Quit it, Goose," said Sam. "I'm so sorry 'bout that. He's used to me and the guys. If he does it again, just holler at him." I smiled. I knew I wouldn't be hollering at Goose.

After establishing how we both knew my friend from college, he rolled down the truck window and let the wind billow the sleeves of his shirt. We climbed the little mountain road from the store to what, I guess, was the town. All I saw was a post office and a few shotgun buildings that could have been a country doctor's office or a dry goods store. A small gas station in the bend of the road had old Shell pumps with the circular logo on the top. I guessed there was a bait shop inside from the looks of a hand-lettered sign on the window.

Sam pulled up in front of a small, white, two-story house that was about a half mile from the town center. Because the flowers behind the old iron fence were so spectacular, you almost didn't notice that the house was in need of repair. Shutters drooped, screens rested on the ground beneath the windows, and the porch boards screamed loudly when we stepped up on them. It also needed a paint job.

"This is Mrs. Wilmer's place," he said. I don't think he had met my gaze since we met. He was quiet, comfortable in his own skin, with no desire to impress me one way or the other. "She has a room upstairs that she rents for $25 a week. That too much for you?"

"No," I said staring through the leaded glass in the old wooden front door. Mrs. Wilmer finally answered our knock. She was a tall, thin, still handsome woman in her late fifties. Sam said she used to be the town librarian.

"Mrs. Wilmer, this is Lora Sinclair from Mississippi. I think she's up here to do a little research on our mountain ways. I thought you might have your room upstairs vacant."

After looking me up and down, Mrs. Wilmer motioned for us to come inside. Her house was small but held the most interesting treasures— a crazy quilt made in the last century to show off the quilters handiwork using wools and brocade on velvet, was draped over the couch in the small parlor. A mandolin rested on a nearby oak table, walls held paintings probably done by local artists, and books rested on every available flat space.

"Follow me." She made her way up the narrow stairs right inside the front door. There were two rooms upstairs and a small bathroom with a pedestal sink and big cast iron tub. "This is it."

Looking over the room, I could have walked back in time, except for the alarm clock on the bedside table. The room looked clean, and the mountain breeze fluttered the old lace curtains in the window.

"I'll leave you two to talk things over," she said as she turned and went back downstairs.

"What do you think, Sam? I don't know anyone here, so I'll have to depend on you for advice. Is she a nice lady, is this a good rate for a room and small bath? Does she supply any meals?"

He smiled and said, "Yes, and you'll have to ask her."

Before I knew it, Sam was carrying my leather satchel and two canvas bags up the stairs. Mrs. Wilmer and I had come to terms on my occupancy.

"Well, I'll be going," he said, putting his hat back on his head where you could see that it had made an imprint in his hair. "Call if you need anything."

"Wait, do you work? What do you do?"

"I teach school, and I carve," he said.

After Sam's truck left in another cloud of dust, I began to unpack. I took out my notebooks that held the research that I'd already done on this area, and placed them on the table by the bed. As I sat down on the bed, it squeaked with the sound of old springs.

I placed my favorite worn, brown cowboy boots near the wardrobe in the corner of the room. This house, like ours at home, didn't have many closets. If it had any, they were small. Finding an empty drawer, I filled it with folded jeans, T-shirts, and underwear. My one simple, black dress, in case I had to go to a meeting or to church, I put in the wardrobe with a few vests and a jacket.

After getting permission from Mrs. Wilmer, I went to a small, black phone in the upstairs hall and called Daddy collect. He answered on the first ring, and gladly accepted the charges.

"Hey there, Lori-girl! Make it OK?"

"Yes sir, I did. I found a room with a nice retired librarian, so you shouldn't have to worry about me getting into much trouble."

"Well, we will see about that," he said. "How long do you think you will stay?"

"Not sure. I'm guessing about six months," I said. "I need to stay until winter so I can see the seasons change. Guess I'll stay as long as it takes. Maybe I'll be home for Christmas."

"That sounds great, sugar. Just be safe, that's all I ask."

"Okay Daddy. I love you. I'll check in every few days to make sure you and Buck are staying out of trouble."

"We will have to see if we can find some trouble," he said, in his quiet, calm manner. We hung up. I couldn't help but worry.

I opened an Atlas I'd brought from home to see exactly where I was in West Virginia and to study the names of some of the neighboring towns. Right before I closed it, the pages fell to the title page.

There under the text was a handwritten "V." It looked fairly recent but not like it was done just yesterday. It was beginning to fade. Just where had I seen that letter before? Was it a "V" or a Roman numeral?

I knew sleep would be hard to come by to-night anyway, and now just thinking about back home and all the things here for me to see will have my wheels turning all night. I don't even have a fan.

Chapter 5
Sam • 1997 • West Virginia

I've lived here all my life, except for the four years I spent in college. The beauty of this place is not something that I take for granted. My parents grew up here but have moved to Kentucky. I see them several times a year. This still feels like home to me.

When I drove Lora around in our little town, and looked at it through her eyes, it must have seemed like 1940 in a hick town to her.

I guess she wonders why we call these mountains, hills. To her, they probably are some pretty big mountains. I really couldn't tell exactly what she was thinking. I hope she

likes it at Mrs. Wilmer's. Sometime Mrs. Wilmer can seem a little cold, but once you get to
know her, she is pretty interesting. She's one
of the few people around here who appreciates
music or art of any kind. I can see that she
might be a good person for Lora to start talking to about mountain culture.

Being a librarian, she was always putting
together a collection of things to get you interested in reading. She asked me one time
to bring a few of my carved pieces to the library for her to put in her wooden case. It's a
long, dark wooden cabinet with curved glass
case that she said came out of a department
store somewhere around here. Just right to go
with my carvings. She mixed my pieces in with
books about carving, art books with pictures
of carvings, books on tree species that would
be good carving wood.

This thing I do with wood has saved my life.
After college, I returned home after hanging
out in the city in bars with music I'd never
heard, drinking hard, and sleeping little. I
needed a job. I sent out resumes, made con-
tacts with people I'd known in class or professors. I guess I always knew that I'd have to find

a day job to support my art, hoping it would make a little money on the side. All artists feel this need to create, to express. The money is nice if it comes along, but we don't count on it.

Teaching art in a small mountain town would be hard to do. Education funding is not great here. Art is one of the first lines to cross off when school people are cutting a budget.

With a minor in history, I did get on at the local school teaching history. After school I teach art—not just to kids, but to anyone who wants to learn. Since I'm partial to carving and sculpture, I have a group that I work with about one day a week. Painters come another day. Sometimes we go to the little store in town to work. Other days they come up here to my cabin to work so they can use some of my tools. Some of my "students" are as young as ten or as old as seventy. I don't care as long as they want to learn—and I learn from them.

While the students work, I work. My pieces are made of wood found deep in the woods— sometimes oak, sometimes cedar. It depends on what kind of carving I want to do. On big pieces, I do power carving, on smaller designs I hand carve. I usually do a little of both.

If I'm really lucky, I might find some walnut. I like for my carving to show the wind, in the flaring of a horse's mane or the sweep of a woman's hair. I like the look of motion. My pieces need to have other elements incorporated in them to make them whole. I used a cypress knee that had already been carved by nature to form a lamp base for a friend of mine who was building a cabin. I just helped it along.

I'm always on the lookout for treasures in these mountains to go with my carvings, rusted wire to form a horse's mane or tail, a piece of metal as an accent, stones for eyes. Sometimes I order special stones that I can't find around here, but I'd rather use the found objects because they help tell the mountain story, and because they are easy on my art budget.

My first impression of Lora was that she seemed like someone I would like. She is interested in her work, and I like that. I wouldn't call her beautiful by model standards, but striking.

She's a tall woman with long legs, long fingers. She wears her dark brown hair in a low-maintenance style—usually pulled up away from her face or braided with the plait hanging down her back. Her eyes are the thing you notice first about her, hazel with little flecks of amber around the pupils. They seem to look right into your soul.

I've noticed that when she is a little nervous she has a habit of playing with the ends of her hair. It's a sweet gesture. Her smile comes easily.

I make these tiny carved, woodland, creatures and hang them from a delicate silver chain. Maybe I'll make her one. Wonder if she would like a fox, deer, bear or owl? I'll have to know her a little better before I know which one she'd like.

I'm not sure she will be up here long. There are a bunch of us guys who went to high school together. Most are like me with my carving. They have day jobs. In our circle, we have a lawyer, timber estimator, carpenter, store owner, and me—the teacher. Some of them came from coal mining families but broke tradition and didn't follow their fathers' footsteps into the mines. We still hang out together, play pool in the back of the store, drink a few beers.

Most of my friends are musicians. On Friday nights, if the weather cooperates, we gather at the store and sit around on the tailgates of our trucks. I listen. They play. Some of the guys are married. One, besides me, is not. The wives usually bring something to cook on an open fire we build in the center of our circle of trucks.

We eat, and then we sit on the tailgates of trucks or in lawn chairs. The wives and other people who are there to listen are wrapped in old blankets or quilts. They sit with their eyes closed as they breathe the scented mountain air and listen to the music.

Goose loves it because he usually gets thrown more than one half-eaten burger or rib. He smiles all night. Maybe Lora would like to listen, too. That might fit right in with her research on mountain culture. I could ask and see what she says.

Chapter 6
Buck • 1997 • Mississippi

As Mr. Asa gets older, he's letting me do more with the farm operations. I still depend on him to tell me what calves to sell, what row crops, if any, to plant. His mind is the same, but his body is just wearing out. Now I drive the truck and he rides shotgun, still in charge and making all the calls.

I keep in touch with Lora and tell her what we are doing down here. She's still up in West Virginia studying those mountain folks and their ways.

Farming has changed so much in the last

few years. Farmers have bigger, fancier trac-
tors and equipment. We have a good tractor but not one of those fancy ones. Mr. Asa
still likes me to ride the fences horseback to
check cows. Every now and then, we will drive
around the pasture in the truck, if the ground
is not too wet.

I go to a little country church not far from
here. The people are real nice, and I fit in good.
I met a girl at church a few months ago. I've
always been a little scared to talk to girls. I'm
afraid they will think I'm not smart. When
Mary Simmons "Simsie" Montgomery walked
into the church with her aunt last summer, I
couldn't quit thinking about her.

Mr. Asa let me ask her to come out here and
go horseback riding. I looked down at my feet
when I asked her if she'd like to come. When
I looked up, she was smiling. Just guessing,
I figured she was a little younger than I am.
I had a few dates in high school, and one or
two after, but never felt this way about anyone. Maybe I never had a reason to look for

someone, 'til now.

So the next Sunday after church, she came home with me. I'd asked Sadie to come to the house on Saturday and cook us something to have for Sunday dinner, and she did. We had country food, my favorite—baked chicken, butter beans, potatoes, cornbread, and chocolate pie. I was worried that Simsie might want something else like pizza or hamburgers, but she said it was all real good.

After lunch, we went out and caught the horses. They were up near the gate by the old corn crib. I think she must have ridden before 'cause she took the bridle from me and threw the reins over the mare's neck to steady her, and held the headstall with her hand up high, over and between the mare's ears. She eased the bit right into her mouth and buckled the throat latch.

We led the horses to the hall of the old barn, and I pulled tack from the room where we keep the saddles and blankets. I offered to saddle her horse, but she said she could do it. After a quick brushing to knock off the dirt and loose hair, she threw the blanket on the mare's back, adjusting it just right on her withers.

We saddled up and off we went, down a little dirt road that runs on the side of the property, back to a pine thicket. I've always been shy, specially 'round women. But the longer we rode, the more I talked. I talked about things I've never told anybody, about my mama, about loving this place and Mr. Asa and Lora, and about how hard it was for me in school.

Simsie is shy but a good listener. After walking the horses hard for about a half hour, until they began to sweat a little, she started talking, too. She was here for the summer, she told me, visiting her aunt and trying to decide what to do next. She's from Tennessee, a little town not far from Memphis. She learned about horses by working after school and on weekends at a stable near her house.

It was her job to muck out stalls, clean and refill water buckets, polish the tack after a day of riding. Sometimes the trainer would send her out in the round pen with a new horse to lunge. She liked that. She said it scared her a little at first. But after working the horse in the round pen about thirty minutes, she would stop and hold out her hand, and the horse would sniff the dirt and gradually walk over to her, licking its lips in a sign of submission, and let her catch it. I reckon' that was a good feeling.

Simsie told me she went to community college for two years to be a nurse. She is trying to figure out whether she wants to go back to school or start working. I wished she would start working here.

That was the first of many horse rides, long walks, and trips to church. She likes music and sometimes we go into town to a little restaurant that has live music. Since we started dating, I've seen movies, eaten at fancy restaurants and even gone dancin'. I'm not real good at that, but I'm gettin' better.

I know I love her. Nobody ever told me loving someone would be this good. Can't imagine she would want to marry me, but I'm hoping she will. I'm just takin' my time. She thinks I'm good looking. I've heard that before, but nobody ever stayed around to find out what I'm really like.

After all that thinking about what to do, Simsie got a small apartment in town and went to work at a local clinic for people who can't afford to go to real doctors or specialists.

I'm proud of her for settling down and doing something so good for the people around here.

After we had been dating awhile, I wrote to Lora and told her all about Simsie and sent a picture of us, so she could see what she looks like. We are by the old farm gate. I'm standing and she's sitting on the top rail. I still can't figure what she sees in me. Her long reddish-brown hair is past her shoulders.

When I kiss her goodnight after we have been somewhere, I have to let her stand on the second step to the porch. The top of her head comes right under my chin. You wouldn't call me a real tall guy. I'm about six feet tall, but she makes me feel like I'm ten feet tall and can protect her from anything bad. I sure want to try.

I can tell if somebody is a good person by the way our cow dogs act around them. This man who lives down the road keeps comin' around snoopin' and asking me if I think Mr. Asa would like to sell off some of this property. I told him I'd ask Mr. Asa. Really don't want to cause it would only upset him. Then this man asks for Lora's address so he can send her something. I haven't given it to him yet. I guess I'll have to talk to the boss after all and tell him about this man and what he wants.

The first time he got out of his fancy truck and came around to the barn where I was stacking square hay bales for the horses, one of the dogs, a border collie, bristled up and was sniffin' all around him, and circling his boots in the dust. Her name is Sister, and she crouched down and put the "stare" on him like she does when she's trying to make a cow stay where she put her.

Sister is mostly white with one black ear and a black eye patch. Those are not perfect markings for a Border Collie, but she has cow in her, according to Mr. Asa. "That's what we are looking for, Buckshot." She's always taken every step Mr. Asa took. Now she follows me, too.

When Simsie got out of my truck the first time, and she and Sister made eye contact, Sister sat at her feet and looked up at her with her ears up. Well, one ear is always up, and the other one flops to the side. But she didn't put them flat on her head. When Simsie spoke to her, she panted and dropped to her stay position. Now she follows Simsie around when she comes to visit.

I called Lora to tell her about the creepy guy down the road, 'bout him wanting to buy some of the land. She said she would talk to her Daddy about it the next time he called, just to be sure.

She said, "Daddy will tell that peckerwood to mind his own business." Peckerwood, that's one of those mountain words she's learned, and I like it.

I bet Mr. Asa thought by now he would have some grandchildren to inherit this land. But Lora is still single and working in the mountains.

Chapter 7
Lora • 1997 • West Virginia

It's been a week now since Sam dropped me off here at Mrs. Wilmer's. I'm beginning to get used to the mountain sounds and smells. Mrs. Wilmer is warming up to me a little. Yesterday I went downstairs to find her working in the corner of her parlor that she uses as a little office area. There is a beautiful drop-leaf secretary desk with cubby holes where she organizes her bills and paperwork.

She has a stunning collection of antique paperweights. This one on her desk is clear with a brilliant purple flower inside. As I came down the stairs, she looked up and smiled. She was wearing faded jeans with a button-down shirt over a T-shirt and her light brown hair was down. She didn't look so formidable.

"Mrs. Wilmer, is this a good time for us to talk?" I asked.

"Oh, sure. And you can call me Helen. Mrs. Wilmer sounds like you are speaking to my mother." We both smiled, and the ice was broken.

"I wanted to tell you a little about what I'm doing here. I think you might be the perfect source to get me started."

"Well, I was a little curious," she says. "Let's get a cup of coffee or tea while we talk." We moved to the small kitchen table while she made the most wonderful-smelling coffee.

"I've been hired to do a linguistic and cultural study comparing the dialects and customs of the people of West Virginia and the people of the South. From what I have seen so far, I can already tell that both regions have a lot in common in breathtaking scenery and good people. I guess I need to get some direction on where to begin."

She stirred her coffee and looked at me as though she was seeing me for the first time.

Maybe she thought I'd just come here for an adventure or to get away from a bad relationship. I'm guessing she might be one of the few college-educated people in this small town with the exception of the few medical professionals and a handful of teachers at the tiny school—and Sam.

"Well, I wasn't expecting that," she said. "I'd suggest you just walk among us for a few weeks and listen. You could go to church with me this weekend. Churches are made up of all kinds of people from all walks of life. You will find our music a little different too. You might go with your friend Sam to one of his Friday night pickings at the store. I'll give this some thought, but I have some ideas. We also had some books at the library that might be good sources."

I could tell I had made a friend. We sat at the table talking until the morning sun moved higher in the sky and our coffee turned cold.

"Tell me your story, if you don't mind sharing it," I said.

Helen took a deep breath and seemed to relax more. She told me that she grew up in this community, married here, returned to work here after graduating from college.

"Steve worked for the power company. It was sometimes a dangerous job. We never knew when he would be called out to fix an outage."

Helen had two children, an infant son who died shortly after birth, and a daughter who was now living in Virginia, near Washington D.C., with a husband and a daughter of her own.

"We were married twenty-five years before I lost my Steve to cancer," she said. "I've known the heartbreak of loss in the deaths of my parents and my son, but nothing compares to losing your mate," she said with a small quiver in her voice.

"This little house belonged to my grandmother. Steve and I lived in a log cabin we built up in the mountains. After he died, I needed to move, so I came here. The cabin is still there, and I still own it. My daughter and her family stay there when she comes home. I go up every now and then to check on things and clean up.

"I always expect to hear the screen door slam and see Steve walk in and sit at the big cedar wood bar to see what I'm cooking for supper. 'Hey baby, what you got going in here,' he'd say. I guess I'm still in love. No need to be looking for anybody else.

"I worked at the library for a few more years and then felt the need to retire. Some days I just couldn't concentrate. Seemed like it got harder and harder to convince people around here to read, especially the young ones. I had summer reading camps and did programs at the school and at churches. 'Like getting blood out of a turnip,' as my mama used to say."

"So what do you do now?" I asked.

"I read, of course," she said with enthusiasm. "I've found a couple of women my age who like to walk. We walk up and down these winding roads close to town about twice a week. You can come with us if you want to.

"Then I joined an artist guild. There are so many talented people in these hills. Some are carrying on a tradition that has been passed down to them for generations and some are new artists, like Sam. I'm not sure what I am yet.

"I'm having to find out what I can and can't do. Quilting is interesting to me, but so is pottery. One member has a kiln at his house.

If someone makes pottery, he takes it home to fire it. We don't need any kiln in that old wooden building. The guild meets in the old school that was right before being torn down. We collected dues and raised money and fixed it up some. I'm trying not to sit still."

"I'm glad we had this talk," I said, taking my cup to the sink and washing it out. "I'll check with Sam and see if I can go to his Friday night pickin'. And I'll just start listening."

Chapter 8
Sam • 1997 • West Virginia

It's Thanksgiving break, and that means I don't have to get up early and go to school. I kick off the covers and look at the end of the bed. Goose raises his head and looks back at me. "We don't have to get up," he seems to be saying to me.

Last night I decided to call Lora to offer to take her to some places that might help her with her project. She thought that was a great idea. I told her I'd pick her up about ten. I looked at the clock by my bed, and the digital dial read 9:15. Putting it into high gear, I jumped out of the bed and called for Goose to come with me to take care of his morning business.

He is already getting gray around his mouth. He's not that old, about five I guess. I got him when Rex's female lab had unexpected puppies. They are full-blooded but weren't planned. I traded a carving in a piece of mahogany that I'd been saving, to Rex in exchange for little Goose. His then-wife wanted a likeness of their beloved dog, a gorgeous chocolate lab with soulful golden eyes. I hope Rex got to keep it after they split. The trade was good on my end.

Goose sure does keep me company. He was about two years old before I really started liking him. Until then, he had chewed two pairs of shoes, my best beat-up and loved cowboy boots, and a wicker basket, just to name a few things. There are scratch marks around the door and all the windows on the porch. I am proud of my cabin and planted azaleas around on the shady side of the yard.

Goose dug dog holes around them. He made trenches, just his size, to lie in to keep himself cool. When the rains came and the dog holes filled with water, he would still lie in them, and as a result, look like a muddy, homeless dog.

He gnawed the corners of my porch swing and shredded every item that was left outside. The year he became six, he began to mellow—and gray.

"Damn dog."

So while Goose is outside looking for squirrels and other creatures to bark at, I'm scrambling around finding semi-clean jeans, boots, and a long-sleeve T-shirt. I rush out the door and tell Goose to "Load up." In the passenger side of the truck he goes, thumping his muddy tail on the leather seats.

Taking a second look at the state of my truck, I run back in and grab a towel and jump the steps all in one leap. I gather all kinds of wrappers and bottles from the floorboard and chunk them in the trash on the way out. My backseat is full of pieces of wood that I've found, scraps of metal, a bucket of rocks, and just plain junk. I'll have to make room for Goose back there when I pick Lora up.

She's waiting for me outside Mrs. Wilmer's house when I pull up. "Ready?" I ask. Didn't count on her bringing things with her. She has a satchel for her computer, yellow legal pad, and a hand-held digital recorder.

"Wow, you are prepared," I say. "I thought we would go over to the store and let you talk to Rex and his mama. You met them the day I picked you up.

"I remember. Do you want to tell me their story?" she said.

"I'd rather they tell you," I said, giving her a wink.

About that time Goose stuck his head between the seats, with his tongue hanging out and panting.

"Oh, Goose! You smell like you've been eating frogs!" Lora said, laughing as he nudged her with his nose. "That doesn't matter at all to me—animal lover from birth. How long have you had him?"

"Oh, he's about five. Can't imagine doing without him. Do you have dogs?"

"We have always had cow dogs on the farm back in Mississippi," Lora said as she stroked Goose's head. "They have jobs, but I love them like pets, too. They are very loyal to their humans. Goose is great. He just needs some manners."

"I guess you're right about that," I said. "Changing the subject, what did you expect to find here in West Virginia?"

"I'm not sure. When you compare the South and the Appalachians, you see that they both have some pretty dismal statistics, like last in median income, last in education scores, poverty, drug abuse. I know since you live here you don't want those to be the impressions I get. I need to see the bad and the good."

I nodded.

"It's hard for me to see the bad things about Mississippi when I see so much good. I know we have areas of poverty, kids who don't score well on standardized tests, even some gang activity. All those things need to be addressed,"

"You're getting worked up," I said. She was smiling at me from across the truck seat.

"Yeah, I guess I am. I'll really get worked up when I tell you about the good stuff."

When we got to the store there were no customers, so Rex and his mama, Jolie Durham, pulled up the rockers by the non-lit fire and invited us to come on over.

"Lora, I think you met Rex the day you came

and his mama, Jolie."

She smiled and Rex offered his hand. "I want to talk to both of you about some of the customs and lifestyles of your state," I said. I would also be listening carefully to their dialect, especially Jolie's, to see how it was different from mine. The sound of their voices was considerably different from my Mississippi accent.

"Mrs. Jolie, did you grow up here?"

"Lordy, yes," she said while untying her apron. "Born and raised right here in this county. My daddy was a coal miner. That right there is a hard life, I'm telling you. He left the house before daylight and was home after dark.

Ain't no wonder so many of those miners get depression working in the dark those hard hours. I always thought that was why he took to drinkin'. Lots of those men who do manual labor start drinkin' to dull the pain. It's hard work, hard on the body."

Mrs. Jolie's diction has a sharper more nasal quality. She doesn't add extra syllables like I do.

More information than I planned on getting

just seemed to spill from her. Rex looked back and forth from her to me to Sam, like he was afraid she was saying too much.

"My daddy got the black lung. It turnt to cancer, and he died when I was still in school. Mama didn't want my brother in the mines, so she moved us here and bought this here store. 'Bout the only jobs around here are mining, working in restaurants, and now there's some tourist trade around the Cranberry River.

"Anyway, she bought the store and ran it 'til she died, and then I started running it. Rex's daddy kept us in food. He hunted and kept us a few cows and a hog or two. We'd feed one to slaughter and put up every year. We had us a garden, too.

"When I started keeping house, mama told me I could make it through the winter if I put up a hundred jars—of something—peas, corn, peaches, blackberries. We had a root cellar where we kept taters and apples. In her day, we even canned meat. Now I just freeze it."

Rex interrupted. "Mama, she may not want to know about all that stuff."

"Oh, but I do," I said. "That's exactly what I want to know about. What do you have to add

Rex?"

"I think we will just let mama talk today, and I'll tell you my story later," he said, looking down at his feet, and then at Sam, making brief eye contact.

"Well, that's okay by me," I said. "Mrs. Jolie, I hope you will let me come talk to you another time. I'm sure I'll think of some questions when I get back to my room."

"Ya'll come on in the back office. I fixed us a little lunch."

A little! She had made chicken-fried deer meat, peas she had canned, mashed potatoes, and a blackberry cobbler from the berries she had put up.

"My goodness, Mrs. Jolie, I wasn't expecting all this," I said, filling my plate with the wonderful food.

"I know you didn't," she said. Her blue eyes twinkling. "I left you a poke full of jelly, jam and a few taters over there by your pocketbook. You and Mrs. Wilmer can have yourself a treat."

After thanking her for the interview and the food, Sam and I hopped up in his truck.

"How bout we just do a little riding and lookin'," said Sam. "I could take you over to see the cranberry glades in Pocahontas County," he said, "and down the river."

It was November, and snow comes early on the mountains. The roads were patchy with ice.

"If we get to stay long enough, I'll treat you to the best hot dog in West Virginia," said Sam. "You wanna come Rex?"

Rex declined, saying he had a new shipment of canned goods to write up and put on the shelves. Off we went.

On the way, I asked Sam why Rex was hesitant to talk.

"Rex is one of the lucky ones, but it came the hard way," he said, looking back in his rear-view mirror.

"There are a lot of people up here that get caught up in the drug thing. You know, it's a cycle, get laid off a job, depression sets in, start with this and it leads to that. Rex was in bad shape this time last year. It cost him a job and a good woman who loved him.

"He finally hit rock bottom and checked himself into a facility. Stayed about six months. It's a battle he faces every day, but so far, he's winning. It's a good thing his mama let him come back here and work with the store. Our little Friday night gatherings have given him something to hold on to."

I nodded silently. To be honest, I wasn't surprised. Rex had a sadness about him that still lingered.

"Speaking of Friday nights, why don't you come this Friday and see what it's all about?"

"Sure," I said. "I was wondering if you were going to let me into the inner circle."

Goose gave me another face slurp, and Sam just shook his head.

Later after touring around, Sam proved he was right. This was not your ordinary hot dog. It was smothered in chili and topped with a mound of homemade coleslaw. I think if you live up here you have to put slaw on everything.

"Wow, I'm full as a tick," I said, pushing the last bit in my mouth.

Sam smiled. "Lora girl, I think you're picking up our lingo."

"Nope," I said patting my full stomach. "I brought that one with me from Mississippi."

Chapter 9
Buck • 1997 • Mississippi

I went in to check on Mr. Asa yesterday morning and found him asleep in his recliner. A pot of water for tea was on the stove and had boiled dry. The stove eye was still burning.

"Mr. Asa, you need to wake up now. Did you take your medicine this morning?"

He pushed his glasses back on his nose and looked at me through groggy eyes.

"Don't feel too good this morning, Buckshot. I think I might just go back to bed. If I don't feel better, I might get you to take me to see Doc in town tomorrow."

"Oh, sure. We can go today if you feel real bad," I said. By the look in his eye I could see that I didn't stand much of a chance of getting him dressed and out to the truck for a trip to town.

"Naw, we'll just go tomorrow. You can call them and see if that's okay. Number's over there by the phone."

After I got him something to drink and back in the bed, I called and made an appointment. Guess I need to call Lora, too, but I think I'll wait 'til after we see the doctor. Tonight I was supposed to go eat with Simsie. Maybe I better call and cancel. I have a feeling I better stay here with him tonight.

After calling Simsie, she suggested that she bring the food over here. She said there would be plenty for everyone.

We had a great meal, just the three of us. After we finished, Simsie went to work in the old kitchen, clearing plates, and storing leftovers. Mr. Asa and I sat at the kitchen table and talked for well over an hour.

"Guess it's time for me to turn in," he said. "Y'all mean the world to me," he said with a faint smile. I nodded.

"After I see Simsie out, I'll come back to spend the night. Like old times, in my old room."

"I'm okay, Buck," he said. But I could tell that he would really be more comfortable with me there.

"Be right back," I said.

I came back and unpacked things I'd need to stay overnight. I checked on Mr. Asa, and he seemed to be resting all right. I got in my bed and listened to the night sounds and the familiar language of the old house.

Trees rustled against the tin roof, the house settled and popped. I could hear an occasional scamper above me in the attic. Must have been a small rodent.

I thought about the times, after working a 12-hour day, I'd fallen asleep in this bed before dark. When you work all day out in the heat, and it doesn't get dark in late July 'til nearly 9 o'clock, it's easy to go to bed before it gets good dark. City guys wouldn't understand that. They would be just getting out to prowl around.

My mind started wandering back to that fellow who keeps asking about the land. His truck was back around the corner today, just riding by, like he's just checkin' on us. He don't scare me a bit. But I'd hate for him to come around here if Lora is home.

As I lay there in the dark, I knew how blessed I'd been to be part of this family, if only on the outside. The day Mr. Asa let me carve my name on the big Beech tree, I actually felt like I might belong. The night sounds put me into a deep, peaceful sleep.

About two in the morning, I woke up suddenly. Had I heard something or just had a bad dream? I lay still in the darkness with my heart beating up a storm. I listened. I heard it again. Then I heard the sound of breaking glass followed by a solid thud. I knew what I'd find.

Running to the kitchen, I found Mr. Asa slumped against the cabinet on the old pine floor. A broken glass was by his hand. I looked into his blue eyes, and there was no one there.

I decided to wait to call Lora, but I did call the sheriff's office to report his death. They told me the coroner would be out at daylight.

Stretching him out on the floor in a resting position, I covered him with one of his mama's quilts. I sat there at that kitchen table, where we had had so many good meals and good talks, and just waited for morning. It was a long time coming.

Chapter 10
Lora • 1997 • West Virginia

This morning I got the call that I've dreaded all my life. Buck called to tell me that Daddy was gone. I just stared at the phone, speechless. So many things ran through my mind all at one time—some important, some trivial.

Who would take care of the farm, who would check on Buck, what about the livestock, was there a will, did Daddy have a nice suit to be buried in, who would go to the funeral home to make arrangements?

After taking several deep breaths, I said, "Buck, was he there by himself?"

"Oh no, I spent the night, and me and Simsie came out and brought dinner. He pretty much seemed himself, just a little peaked and tired."

"Oh good. I'm glad you were with him. I'm going to see what kind of flight I can get and will try to be there by tomorrow. Tell the funeral home I'm coming, and you and I can make arrangements. I'll be in touch."

After staring at the floor in a blank state for several minutes, I waited for tears to come. They were nowhere near the surface yet. Why hadn't I been there more often? I asked myself a lot of questions as I got my things together.

I asked Helen if I could borrow her car to go see Sam. Maybe he would take me to the airport, about forty-five miles away. She agreed and gave me a big hug. That brought the tears up a few notches.

Knowing Sam would be at home since school hadn't started, I drove slowly up to his mountain cabin.

I found him in his shop just starting on a piece of cottonwood. When I got out and walked in the door, he did a double take when he saw me, and stood to greet me.

"I got a call this morning that my Daddy has died. When I get a plane ticket, do you think you could take me to the airport?"

He looked at me a minute and reached for my hand. I took it and ran my fingers over the callouses caused by countless hours of carving. I traced every one. Then he pulled me into his arms.

"I'll do whatever you want me to do," he offered, his voice deep with emotion. Taking a step closer, I wrapped my arms around his neck. The tears came and didn't stop.

He guided me over to a big rocking chair and eased me into his lap. We just sat there for a long time. He just held me and rocked me and let me cry. No words were spoken.

When I did get up, he smiled down at me. "Call me when you get your plans made. I'll take you. Do you want me to fly home with you?"

"No, I need to take care of business. I'll have to go back before long, and then I want you to go and see the farm. Things will have calmed down by then."

He bent and kissed me lightly on the cheek. "You're a good man, Sam Wood," I said.

"I've been practicing for when I needed to be," he said.

I walked out of the shop, letting the old wooden screen door shut behind me, and drove down the mountain to Helen's house. It's amazing what a little rocking will do when your heart is breaking.

Chapter 11
Buck • 1997 • Mississippi

I knew sooner or later Lora would come home. Since Mr. Asa died, I've been keeping the place up. He trusted me with his cows and to get the hay cut. Every time I haul calves to the sale, I deposit the money in the farm account and send Lora the receipt. She keeps up with the business side.

She still pays me what Mr. Asa paid me, which isn't much, but I don't need much. If we have a money-making year, she sometimes gives me a bonus at Christmas. I've been saving that extra money.

After I got older, I moved back into the house mama and I had. I've fixed the porch, painted the outside. Looks pretty good. I'm not much for decoratin', but I have what I need.

When Lora told me she would be here a week from Tuesday, I started clippin' pastures and gettin' ready. She don't criticize how things look, but I didn't want her to have a reason to.

I guess I could do better for myself, but I love this place and feel like it's where I'm supposed to be. I quit school in the 10th grade. Just couldn't keep up. Mr. Asa got me to go to these classes at the library in town where this nice lady helped me get my GED in case I ever have to go work in town. That lady was real patient with me. It took about a year and a half, but I'm glad I did it, and it made Mr. Asa proud.

Things might be different around here if Lora stays. Or if she ever gets married. She's too busy with her work right now to think about a man, I guess. She hasn't been up in the mountains of West Virginia long. I don't know exactly what she does. All I know is she takes all this electronic equipment up there and records the way people talk.

Maybe she will do that down here in Mississippi. I've been told that I talk funny. When I went on a trip to St. Louis with my class before I quit school, some of the other kids laughed at the way I talk. I don't sound different to me.

The cow herd is looking good. Hope she will be pleased with that too. We have about a hundred commercial cattle—black and white face, Hereford cross, and some red cows. Mr. Asa didn't think too much of raising those fancy purebred cattle. But he sure knew how to work a bunch of cows. Always slow and quiet with them.

"Buck, ease up behind that heifer and see if you can move her through that gate." It paid off. His cattle didn't scatter. If he wound up with a crazy cow, she would go to the sale pretty soon.

"If the mama is wild, chances are the calf will be, too," he said. He would go out late in the afternoon in his old truck and just park in the pasture while they came up to the window for him to give them some range cubes right out of his hand. I try to do that too, but I'm not as good at it as he was.

With nobody really living in the house, I

guess I better clean up there a little too. It sorta looks like a man has been living in here. Mr. Asa had one of the original big rooms. He pretty much stayed in there most of the time. It still has the furniture he and Lora's mother picked out all those years ago. He did add a recliner last year. He put it up next to the heater.

The floor in his room is that old linoleum that is printed to look like a multi-colored carpet. It has worn spots up close to the heater and at the side of his bed. Guess you can look at the floor and see the path that has been traveled over time. Lora would probably like to get the floor back to just wooden planks. Maybe I can talk to her about doing that when the time is right.

After a long day of work, Mr. Asa would wash up, kick off his boots, find something easy for supper, and then get out his books. He didn't even have a TV in his room. That man read more books than I can imagine reading in a lifetime. I never read just to read. It's too hard for me. I can read what I need to. Most of the time I can figure out things on my own.

I'm just not going to read a book just for fun like Lora does. She used to spend hours with her nose in a book. Mr. Asa would send her to the barn to do chores, and I'd find her later up in the hay loft reading.

"You better get your nose outa that book and start working before your daddy finds out you haven't done what he told you," I'd say. She would just stick her tongue out at me and keep reading. But somehow, she would hurry and get her chores done before Mr. Asa found out she hadn't been working all that time.

Chapter 12
Lora • 1997 • Mississippi

When I left Memphis International Airport at six in the evening and hit the pavement to find my rental car, I felt like I'd stepped into a fog of humidity. The weather in Mississippi changes with a heartbeat. One minute it is crisp and cool, and before you know it, you feel drenched in humidity—even in the winter. It's been so long since I'd been back home that there were a lot of things I hadn't thought about for a while. There is a particular, humid smell around dusk, making the small hairs at my temple curl when I didn't want them to.

Then there is the kudzu. When you don't see it every day, it's easy to forget. That troublesome vine imported from Japan in the 1940s was intended to prevent erosion of the soil. It is sleeping now. Its brown leaves and vines covering roadsides and banks for miles around.

Those who aren't familiar with it are always struck by its eeriness as it creeps over fence posts, finally pulling them down. If left unattended, it winds its way through ditches and gullies. It is plentiful on our place.

When I was little, I tried to imagine what the tall vine-covered telephone poles looked like from a distance—like trying to find poodles or bears in the clouds. Asa used to say that if a cow stood still too long, the kudzu would be up to its udders by suppertime. Sometimes the kudzu-covered poles and trees looked like a Mississippi version of the Christ of the Ozarks up in Arkansas, extending his giant out-stretched hands. Sometimes you can see the grim reaper. The vines make a perfect and inviting blanket of the ditches they were meant to cover.

What the non-Mississippian might not know was that the leaves on those vines were scratchy, not velvety smooth as they appeared. And they covered things you didn't want to see, like old car carcasses, rotting fence posts, skeletons of dogs that didn't make it across the highway. The vines provided a haven for snakes and other critters.

But there were things I remembered about Mississippi that I didn't see, hear, or smell— no Bob White quail calling in the distance, no scarcely-traveled one-lane corridors covered by canopies of tree branches, no smell of wood smoke from the small family houses on the farm.

When I exited the interstate in North Mississippi on the way to my old home place, I noticed the stores, a McDonalds, Wal-Mart, places I could see from any small stop off the highway in any town in the country. From this viewpoint, it was generic, without the small, Southern charm that I remembered from my childhood.

I was coming home. Not the kind of home-coming one welcomes. The kind that happens when all relatives are gone and you are the one left to tie up the loose ends, to clean out the house, make financial decisions, box up photos and paperwork, put an end to an era, and a way of life. Maybe I won't have to sell the farm if Buck and Simsie want to stay there for now.

I turned off the main highway onto the gravel road leading to the house where I grew up. The long, narrow driveway to the house was bordered on each side by barbed wire fences, held up by cedar trees or posts They were cut deep in places where the trees had grown around wire that was strung forty years ago by Asa and hired help on the place.

My granddaddy never asked the workers to do anything he didn't ask of his son, as well. Asa must have been not much older than fifteen when he stood shoulder-to-shoulder with the workers, carefully digging holes for posts where there were no trees for support.

They sweated as they stretched the wire and attached it to the trees with staples. Now the wire sagged and the trees were scarred. It provided enough barrier to keep in the few cows that still grazed in those side pastures.

Expecting the house to be in a sad state of neglect, I was pleasantly surprised to find a neatly-trimmed yard. Even if there wasn't much in the way of landscaping around the house, it looked pretty good for a home that hadn't had a woman's touch in years.

Daddy had been there by himself, except for Buck, since I left home to go to college. When I was old enough to take care of myself, Shelly went back to Memphis where she reentered college and found a career. She had put those things on hold to be with us when I was little, and I loved her for it.

One of the disadvantages of being an only child is that you are left alone to put things in order. Only-child life when you're little is pretty good. You don't have to worry about who sits in the front seat, who gets the biggest piece of pie.

Although you might say I had Buck around to compete with me, but his sweet nature usually gave in to my wishes. When your parents get old, it falls to you to make decisions, keep them on track with medical appointments, and feel guilty about not being there. I was lucky that I had Buck to help with some of the things I couldn't do long distance.

You are the one who inherits the task of closing the home. That sounds so cold and matter of fact. There are legal issues to settle, documents to go through, furniture to sell or keep, and memories to sort.

After dropping my bags and project notes on a still-beautiful but worn leather armchair in the hallway of the house, I looked around. The refrigerator was clean, mostly bare, but held a few necessities, like milk, bottled water, eggs, cheese, and a package of lunch meat that must have been for Buck.

Everything seemed in order. It was like Daddy just cleaned up the kitchen and left to go check cows. Nothing was different. I took my things to my bedroom and sat down on the old quilt that served as my bedspread. Running my hand over it, I noticed that some of the seams were getting raveled.

I'd fallen in love with old quilts when I was about ten. That was the year I had the flu. My eyes hurt and my head hurt. Reading was not an option, and there was no TV in my room. I pulled the quilt up to my chin to help with the chills that were taking over my body. I ran my hands over every block of that quilt, looking at the different old fabrics, and wondering if those pieces were once an apron or a house dress or a Sunday dress.

Fabric stores were not around when this was made in the early 1930s. This was a friendship quilt made by some of my older relatives. They brought scraps for their block and embroidered their names on it. My great aunt had pieced the Grandmother's Fan quilt top, and all the ladies had sat in the hall quilting it on a frame. I wish I'd been around to hear some of their conversation in 1930.

It was early October and warm for this time of year. Winter months sometimes make sleep hard to find. This house had gas heat, so there were sometimes sounds of a furnace coming to life. With no central air, we depended on the window units in the summer, and they lulled you to sleep. Not tonight.

This particular night the temperature is mild. There is no need for a fan, but not cold enough for the furnace to be running. I turn on a fan anyway to sing its hypnotic song as it stirs the curtains and causes stray paperwork to flutter. There is no moon tonight, so there are no sounds of dogs barking at their own shadows. The crickets are quiet. The frogs are asleep. Leaves have fallen making a sound barrier around the house.

My mind would not quit. How would all this look to someone new, who didn't grow up here, who didn't love the house and barn, the pastures, the history like I did? It might not feel romantic and magical at all. It might feel like a rundown old farmhouse with a lot of unused land.

As the room becomes cooler, I pull up the quilt to my chin and finally drift off to sleep in the house where I grew up. It just didn't seem natural. It was too silent.

Chapter 13
Lora • 1997 • Mississippi

When I woke up this morning, I felt the absolute loneliness. My parents were gone as well as my grandparents. I was officially an orphan. I threw on an old sweatshirt and jeans and headed for the kitchen. There I saw Buck and a pretty girl sitting at our old kitchen table, looking down into their cups of coffee and saying nothing. When I came in, they looked up.

"You must be Simsie," I said to the girl. Buck hugged me and beamed with pride introducing us. "Sorry it has to be a sad time for our first meeting."

She seemed shy, but was happy and interested in everything we had to say, and that was a lot. We sat at the table, where many family gatherings were held, and talked.

"Buck, do you want to go with me to the funeral home?"

"Well, if you want me to. I don't know what I'd have to do with anything," he said, looking over at Simsie.

"You were like a son to him and his companion, and I want your input on what we do."

He seemed surprised and a little touched by my offer.

We planned a simple service, fitting for a man who expected no fuss. I greeted friends as they filed by Buck and me as we stood at the front of the little church where I'd grown up. Some I remembered from childhood, others were new to me. I was glad to see a few of Buck's high school friends there to express sympathy to him. As I sat stoic at the ceremony, I knew the shock would hit later. It did.

Following the funeral, crowds of people came to the farm, more food appeared. I needed to go to bed. Simsie and Buck put the food in containers and stored it in the refrigerator.

"I think I'll come back a little later, Buck, to take care of his business and deal with the house. I want you to just carry on. Do what you're already doing. I'm proud of you for how you have helped him these past few years.

"I think maybe you should come back to stay here in the house while I'm gone. Will that be a problem for you?"

"Oh, no," he said. "I'd kinda like to move back into my old room. It's okay down at my little house, but kinda sad, too. This house is where all the good memories are. I figure I might need some of them memories over the next few days."

He turned his head, but not before I saw a few tears welling in his eyes. I retired to my bedroom. I was tired, and, I'm sure still in shock.

As I reached into the wardrobe that was recessed into the wall across from the one bathroom in the house to get a towel, I noticed the letter "V" carved on the door. I puzzled for a minute trying to think who could have done it or what it could have stood for. My mind was busy enough without this. I was in no shape to solve mysteries tonight. I just let it go.

Crawling in the room that I'd slept in for my first twenty years of life gave me a sweet sense of comfort. The music of this old house and the sounds on its tin roof were alive tonight, and sleep came easier.

The next morning, I found Buck at the horse barn. There were only three horses left on the farm—two were getting on in years but still ridable. I greeted my old friends with the horseman's handshake—extending my hand palm up for them to smell. They inhaled deeply and blew a little puff into my hand.

Buck had cross-tied daddy's old sorrel mare in the hall of the barn while he cleaned her stall. "Lora, I'm thinking about asking Simsie to marry me," he said.

"I'm not surprised to hear that, Buck," I said, giving him a quick pat on the shoulder.

"Not sure she will say yes. She's smarter than I am. She probably makes more money than I do. But I think we can make it if we are careful."

I couldn't help but smile. "Buck, in my opinion, she'd be crazy to say no to the best-looking, hardest-working, sweetest guy in this county. Let me know how it comes out."

He smiled to himself while he continued his barn chores. His blue-gray eyes were sparkling. Buck made a quick head movement to shake his hair out of his eyes. I've seen him make that gesture a thousand times. I bet even if he gets a haircut, he will still do that.

I grabbed a nearby push-broom and began cleaning the barn hall. It felt good to be there with Buck, in the barn, with the horses. The morning sun was moving on up in the sky.

I paused and listened as the horses chewed their morning hay. Dust particles shimmered in the early morning sunlight coming through the Eastern barn windows. A new black and white barn cat, walked back and forth above my head on the rafters, waiting for his feed. For a moment all seemed calm and good. Even though I was sad, I felt a deep comfort to be back in my old surroundings.

I opened the tack room door and looked over the saddles that were stacked neatly on the saddle racks. They were a little dusty but in good shape for their age. I closed the door so I could sweep the old wooden floor. When I reached to open the door again, I saw a small

"V" scratched on the lower part of the door.

What in the world did this mean? Who had access to all these private places? Only Buck. But what did the "V" mean? I couldn't think of a thing.

"Buck, did you see that little letter scratched in the back of the tack room door?"

He looked up, surprised. "What? Don't know what you are talking about Lora."

With that, he busily resumed his chores.

Chapter 14
Sam • 1997 • West Virginia

I've had time to do some thinking since Lora left. This could be the start of something for us. Then again, maybe I was just there when she needed someone. She's not like most girls I've known who hinted that they wanted you to call them or ask them about getting together.

She seems so independent. That little glimpse of her vulnerability was the first I've seen of real emotion in her. I think she likes it up here—the morning mist of the mountains, the lazy curl of smoke from some of the old cabins. Hell, I think she even likes Goose. I guess he gets tired of my company.

I like the way she can look pretty in just a pair of old jeans, boots, and a button-down shirt with her hair braided and hanging over one shoulder. She fits here, seems to me.

I do wonder if she gets bored up here. She has been to college, worked in big cities, dealt with educated people. But somehow, I just can't see her in corporate America.

School started up here in the last of August. I can't believe we are almost at the end of the first semester. In the fall I usually teach American History, West Virginia History, and Civics. This makes my fifth year teaching, so I pretty much know my stuff.

We go over current events every day. I like to try to keep these kids in touch with the rest of the country. Keeping up with news and technology is a hard thing for some of them. For others, it comes easy.

I can tell when they are beginning to get bored with regular classroom lectures. Sometimes we go out and visit rural areas and talk to the old timers about customs and traditions. The older students take recorders or take notes when they do their interview. I pick the best ones to go in the school newspaper.

It does my heart good to listen to the inter-action between the kids and the elders. Last year, one of our girls interviewed a lady in her eighties who still makes corn husk dolls. That's all they had to play with when she was little. Now she does it to keep her mind and arthritic fingers with swollen knuckles busy. She sells the dolls at the little craft fairs that are held up here and at welcome centers across the moun-tains. Any little girl who will be still for an hour is welcome to sit on the corner of her porch while she shares her craft.

The guys like to listen to tales of the old min-ers. Even if they come from a mining family, they sit wide-eyed while the old guys talk of the horrors of the mines in their time, and the bonding camaraderie they had with their co-workers and their families. I need to take Lora on some of those trips. That would fit right in with what she's doing.

School holidays are a little different here than they are for most kids. We close for Labor Day and on the first day of rifle deer season. I guess Lora was surprised about that. Closing for that day is pretty much a tradition here.

Schools have made it part of their calendars for decades.

I understand that in Mississippi, decades ago, the African American schools closed for cotton picking time. Parents and older children picked cotton by hand in the hot Mississippi sun. Machines, advancements in farming, and social changes put that to an end. It was still the same idea—providing for your family.

So many young men hunt, not only for sport, but to supplement their family's food supply through the winter. The last principal we had scheduled a big school event on that first day of deer season, and there was almost a riot. He didn't understand.

Most of the guys will pack up on the weekend and head for the camps and be ready at daylight. Some schools usually let students off a day or two, but faculty and staff report for in-service training. I like to hunt as much as the next guy, but I'm not obsessed with it like some of them are.

I usually spend that first day hunting, too—for unusual wood, found objects. I have to be careful and wear orange, or I could end up stuffed and mounted. Goose always goes with me, and I put an orange hunting vest on him, too.

Today Goose and I are just sitting on the deck of my cabin. It is kind of a deck and dock. Sometimes I fish, sometimes I just take my coffee out there in the mornings and watch the sun peep up over the mountains or go down at night. Many times I return as night falls and listen to the music of the mountains. People around here call this terrain "hills," but we know better.

Lora called early today and asked me to pick her up at the airport, so she wouldn't have to get a taxi to bring her all the way out here. I think my heart may have skipped a beat.

That little flutter scared me a little. So I packed up Goose, scraped the sacks of food and pop cans off the front seat, and headed down the mountain.

When she came through the gates at the terminal, she gave me a sweet and still-a-little-sad smile. I met her and took her bags and gave her a quick hug. We didn't say much on the way back to my truck. I had left it locked with the windows cracked because Goose was in it, waiting for my return. As we approached the truck, we noticed wet nose prints on all the windows. She laughed.

On the way up the mountain she began to talk a little. "That was really hard," she said.

"I'm sure it was. How did you find everything?"

"Good," she said. "Buck had taken care of everything."

"Buck?" I asked.

"I thought I'd mentioned him before. He came to live with us when he was five and has been there ever since. He's been Daddy's shadow all these years. Now he's doing a really good job of keeping the farm running. He even has a girlfriend. I was afraid he might not ever have one. Buck is a little shy, but he is as good as gold. I have really depended on him to take care of things."

I thought for a moment before asking anything else. I didn't want to pry. But I just jumped in and asked anyway. "Do you think you'll sell the farm or move back?"

She looked out the window for a moment before speaking. "Not sure," she said. "I can't imagine selling it. Buck says there is a creepy guy that keeps coming around asking about buying all or part of it. I'm afraid he will use some scare tactics on Buck, and I don't know how he will react to that.

"I will probably go back later to finish taking care of business, the will, look at the finances. By then some time will have passed, and maybe I'll have a clearer head."

I wanted to ask her if she wanted me to go with her, but decided to wait and see how things were going to play out with us.

"Tonight is Friday. Do you want to go to the store and listen to some music?"

"I think that might just be what I need," she said, smiling. "I need to go check in with Helen to unpack and just rest a while. That okay?"

"You, bet!" I think I might have grinned.

I looked in the rearview mirror and Goose was smiling and thumping his tail on the seat.

I wrinkled my nose. "Do you ever give this dog a bath?"

"Sure," said Sam. "He runs through the creek every morning."

Chapter 15
Lora • 1997 • West Virginia

When I climbed the stairs to my little room at Helen's house, I felt a huge relief. It felt good to be back here, with these folks, away from sadness, not worrying about the business side of the farm back home.

Helen came out to meet me when I got out of Sam's truck and gave me a big hug. She's not a real hugging type, so it meant a lot.

I unpacked my bag and headed to the bathroom for a long soak in the cast-iron tub. As the hot water began to make a mist on the mirror in the small room, my tension began to ease.

Finishing my bath, I dried off and put on my favorite old ratty robe and went back to my room. I found a note from Helen taped to my bedroom door. "You have had several calls from Mississippi. Feel free to return the call," it read.

Buck answered on the first ring. "Lora, you won't believe what happened!"

"Are you okay? Simsie okay?"

"Simsie was coming up to the house for supper tonight, and she saw something white off to the side of the road." He was running out of breath as he talked. "She pulled over, rolled down the window, and it was Sister! She'd been shot!"

"Oh, no, Buck! Is she dead?"

"No. Simsie came and got me, and we scooped Sister up and took her to the vet. Doc Henshaw met us at his office. She had been shot in the hip. It wasn't no hunting accident either. Doc said it looked like a .22 bullet. She was lucky, but the wound was deep. He said he wanted to give her time to heal from the inside out. If it didn't heal, he'd have to take her leg."

Buck was almost in tears, and so was I. Sister was the sweetest dog we ever had. She was part of the farm operation.

"And, that's not all," he said. "Simsie said when she drove off the man who has been asking about the property was driving away, and he just nodded and waved a finger at her. Found out his name is Ben Hubbard. He bought the old Winslow place down the road."

"Did you report this to the sheriff?" I asked.

"That's why I wanted to call you. Do you think I should be the one to call?"

"Yes I do, Buck. You and Simsie will have to fill out a report. Find out what you can about Mr. Hubbard. I'll take care of the vet bills. Do the best you can for her. I'll call you tomorrow and check on how things are going. Are you staying at the house?"

"Yes, since Mr. Asa died. I thought that's what you told me to do."

"I did. Are you afraid?"

"No, I'll be okay. I can pick Sister up tomorrow and keep her in the kitchen and look after her."

"Now calm down, Buck. You have done everything just right. Sister is getting the care she needs. You and Simsie did a good job."

We said goodbye, and I hung up. Tears immediately stung my eyes. The thought of someone hurting that sweet dog to get to me or Buck, was horrible.

Boy, that's enough to knock the wind out of your sails. Wait 'til I tell Sam. As much as he likes dogs, he will be fighting mad.

I did tell Sam, and I did get the reaction I expected.

"What kind of person does that?" he said, slamming the heel of his hand on the steering wheel.

"Someone like Ben Hubbard," I said. "I know a guy with the sheriff's department back home and got him to run a background check on him. Nothing serious, but shady. He has bought property down the road from us. If he can get me to sell him our property, he will have road frontage and can put in a development."

"What else did the report say?" asked Sam.

"He had some DUIs, couple of bounced checks that landed him in court. They were pretty big and involved a property deal.

"I feel bad for Buck. He usually does really good, but something like this will agitate him.

I'll check on him tomorrow. In the meantime, let's go hear some music."

Sam smiled and the tension immediately evaporated.

Chapter 16
Sam • 1997 • West Virginia

I've been looking forward to this night. I wanted to introduce Lora to my friends. She's already met Rex. Hope she likes the other guys and their wives. Her news about Sister made me sick. It also scared me a little—for Buck and Simsie, and for her.

We drove up to the store just as the sun was slipping behind the mountains, leaving that beautiful orange fringe above the trees and hills. I could already smell the fire. We parked and Goose jumped out of the truck and took his place in the bed of the truck after I let the tailgate down. I hate to tell Lora, but SEC football fans in the South ain't got nothing on us tail gaiting up here in the mountains.

Lora followed me as I joined the group. I introduced her to Mason and Sophia Harper. Mason plays a rare Gibson mandolin that belonged to his granddaddy. You can tell it has been loved and played hard by all who have owned it.

Easton and Abigail Cade are native to this area. Easton says he is a descendant of some of the original pioneer families. He looks the part, too. Easton might be a good looking guy under those overalls without that long hair parted down the middle and hanging down his back. His beard looks like it hasn't been trimmed in a while.

He's one of the nicest guys around, and his wife is a perfect fit for him. Most importantly, he's a hell of a guitar player. It's not unusual for him to bring several guitars to try out at one of our Friday night pickins'.

There are others that wander in and out to play upright bass, mountain dulcimer or sing. I could sit here on the truck bed and just people watch for hours.

Rex and I round out the regular crowd.

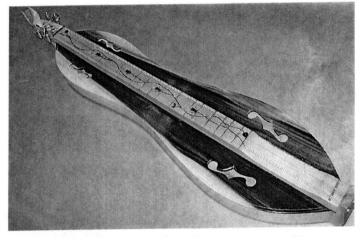

This is an example of a mountain dulcimer, made by Warren May in Berea, Kentucky. (warrenmay.com)

From somewhere unknown people just show up. People from all walks of life drive up, drop their tailgates, and start playing. Some play in their own small groups, while others walk around and sit in to improvise with people they never met.

The atmosphere is something I've never experienced before. Warm, sweet, calming. I look forward to Friday nights. By the end of the night, one group or the other, or a combination of groups, will end up using the front porch of the store as their stage as they bring down the night with some great mountain singing and picking.

Things were just getting started. I walked Lora around and let her watch the different groups playing. Most of the guys played guitar, and there were fiddle, mandolin, and banjos pickers, too. Voices had a mountain twang to them, not country and not exactly Bluegrass, but a sound all its own.

Lora looked amazed. She also looked beautiful in jeans, boots with a native American-inspired poncho in brilliant fall colors draped over her shoulders. This time of year, after sunset, the air really takes on a chill.

We went back to the fire where Rex and the ladies were cooking some sausages. There were bowls of the famous mountain coleslaw, and homegrown vegetables including an onion-like ramp that is a favorite here. Two sawhorses held two wide planks covered by an old, red and white table cloth. On it were biscuits, cakes, and pies. The smell of the sausages and some deer meat cooking was intoxicating.

"Wow," said Lora. "This is as good as a homecoming Sunday at a Mississippi church!"

After talking awhile and eating all we could hold, we went back to the truck to sit on the tailgate. I had spread an old Ohio Star quilt with red and blue blocks in the truck bed, and we climbed up and sat there drinking in the night and the music.

From the sounds of some of the crowd, it seemed like a little Mountain Moonshine might be going around. We had shared a bottle of red wine earlier in the evening, and now the night was looking pretty good from the bed of my truck.

The air turned colder and I saw Lora shiver. We sat with our backs touching, looking up to the stars for a long time. I reached for her hand, and she traced the callouses like she had before.

Then I felt her lean into me and relax. We sat there 'til the quilt was damp with dew and the fire was dying. Goose had rested his head on her leg, let out a big dog sigh, and gone to sleep.

"Want to go now?" I asked. The band guys were packing up their instruments and wiping them off with care.

"Not sure I ever want to go," she replied and linked her arm in mine.

Chapter 17
Simsie • 1997 • Mississippi

I don't like upset, and things around here lately have been upset. Mr. Asa dying was one, then that suspicious guy down the road, and then Sister. The good upset is that Buck finally asked me to marry him.

It's hard to describe the love I have for him. I know he has limitations, but don't we all? He is incredibly good to all he meets—people as well as animals, and especially me. I've never had anyone make a fuss over me. He makes a big fuss!

We enjoy just being with each other. It

doesn't hurt that he is such a beautiful man with his tanned arms, blue-gray eyes, and that untamed thick, blonde hair. Sometimes I don't know what he sees in me.

I've had a good time introducing Buck to things he's never done and places he's never been. As good as the Sinclair family was to him, he never had many opportunities outside the farm.

Last Saturday we went to a small rodeo that was in town. He loved it. We ate homemade hamburgers, pieces of cake, and iced tea from the concession stand and walked around to the back of the arena to look at the bucking stock—horses and bulls.

When that pretty girl came riding into the arena on that good-looking black horse, running full speed, with the American flag flying behind her, I saw a tear run down Buck's face.

He didn't want to miss a single minute of the performance, barrel racing, calf roping, steer wrestling, bareback bronc riding, saddle bronc riding and the big event, bull riding. It was so scary, I had to shut my eyes a few times. Buck took it all in with excitement.

We like to go to movies, and I hope one day

to get him to a museum. We'd have to go to Memphis or Jackson to do that. Simple things are good, too. We like to walk down the quiet country lane near sunset and to sit in the old porch swing with Sister at our feet.

Speaking of Sister, the vet finally removed the drain tube from her hip wound and said she was healing nicely. She was so good about letting me clean the wound. I thought we might have to put one of those funny-looking cones on her head to keep her from gnawing at the bandage, but after a few scoldings, she left it alone, most of the time. Maybe we should let her have a litter of pups. We might need a replacement from her bloodline down the road.

I guess I better start planning a wedding. Buck wants us to get married at our church not far from here. The first time I went to that church with my aunt, I was stunned by its beauty and simplicity. It's a little white church that sits up off the ground on concrete pillars. According to Buck, Mr. Asa said it might be at least a hundred years old.

Last year the men in the church did a little work on it, painting, replacing rotten wood around the windows. They hired a contractor to look at some issues with the foundation. When I walked in before the renovation, I almost felt like I was on the deck of a ship. The floor dipped and sagged in places and was getting dangerous.

Contractors were able to save most of the wide-plank heart-pine floors and stabilize the foundation. I love the windows. They aren't fancy stained glass but look like they were made from old glass. As they became broken over the years, they were replaced with other old glass. Some are wavy; some have bubbles; a few are tinted green; and one in particular has a stamped pattern. The result is a beautiful rainbow of light that spills over the pews just about the time the preacher is getting to the end of his sermon.

One Sunday we strolled out in the little cemetery that is next to the church. Some of the tombstones are really works of art. Little lambs rest on the graves of children, sweet sayings are carved into the stone of a young wife, an angel bends over the resting place of a woman who lived a long life. Some graves go back to Civil War times.

It's really hard to read the words on some

of the old markers. The cemetery is bordered by beautiful rusted fleur-de-lis wrought iron fencing. Many of the older family plots are enclosed with similar but less ornate versions of this fence.

You don't really see the art in gravestones today. I think it is a beautiful, peaceful place with its old cedar trees and the cast iron fence. The most recent grave in the cemetery was that of Asa Vincent Sinclair. Buck stood looking down at it. "Don't seem real, does it?" he said and turned away. I walked behind him looking at the graves of Asa and his wife Beth and his parents, all marked with beautiful but simple monuments.

As we walked toward the gate to leave, we saw many double markers for couples. "Buck, do you know who your daddy is?" I'd wanted to ask that question many times but was afraid to open a dark hole in his heart.

"No," he said sadly. He shook his hair back from his face. "Mama just always said I didn't have a daddy. I was too little when she left to ask her about it," he said.

"What about your mama? Do you want to go see her? I'll go with you. When we get married, do you want her to be here?"

"I hadn't thought about it, really," he said, looking a little sad. I reached up and brushed a stray lock of hair off of his forehead.

"Why don't you write to her and send her a picture of us? We could send the one like the photo we sent to Lora. Do you still have her address?"

"I guess," he said. "The last time I had a letter from her was about two years ago. I can try the same address. I'll think about it."

"I'll do a search on the computer and see if that is still a good address," I offered. "My brother will have to walk me down the aisle since my daddy is gone," I said, picking the seed head off a tall blade of grass.

"My mother will come. Tennessee isn't that far away. There are some nurses at the clinic who I'd really like to be there. Especially Jerica. We've gotten to be pretty close. It will still be a small wedding. Is that okay with you?"

"I don't really care who comes to the wedding except for Lora, Shelly, your family, a few people from church—and you!" he said, playfully pinching me and smiling his beautiful smile.

We dropped the subject.

Chapter 18
Sam • 1997 • West Virginia

I got out of school early today. I thought I'd go by Mrs. Wilmer's and see if Lora wanted to ride to the store. I wanted to see what all she has been recording and writing.

When she got in the truck, she got her usual kiss from Goose and a pat on the shoulder from me. I think it should be the other way around, but I'm waiting for a signal. She told me about some interviews Mrs. Wilmer had set up for her tomorrow with members of a quilting club that takes turns meeting in the homes of the members. Quilting is a handed-down tradition up here. I've seen everything from scrap quilts to some of the modern machine quilting that has been hanging in the library. It all tells a story.

I pulled up at the store. We got out of the truck and left Goose there on the front porch. Mrs. Jolie was behind the register.

"Want a pop?" I asked Lora.

"Sure, but back home we call everything carbonated a Coke, even if it's a Pepsi. But I'll take a real Coke in a bottle," she said, smiling as she looked at the old-fashioned items collected in the glass display case.

"Where's Rex?" I asked.

"Oh, he wasn't feelin' too good today," said Mrs. Jolie. She wrinkled her nose and looked directly in my eyes. "Stayed home."

After seeing if Lora wanted anything else from the store, we jumped back in the truck, and I found myself driving along the narrow mountain road to Rex's house.

"Where are we going?" asked Lora.

"I think I'll pay ole Rex a surprise visit. His mama said he was at home—not feeling too good."

I wanted Lora to see the beautiful leaves as they turned their magical fall colors. The view from this high mountain road was spectacular. But I also wanted to check on Rex. Last Friday night at the store he was a little jumpy. He said he hadn't been sleeping good and brushed me off when I asked him if anything was wrong.

"Do you think Rex is happy here running the store?" Lora said. Her hand had drifted to the back seat where she could scratch Goose behind his ears. I could hear his tail thumping.

"You know, I'm not sure," I said, giving this topic some thought. "Rex is a smart guy. He may be getting a little bored." I told her that I'd noticed him being a little anxious Friday night.

She nodded her head. "I didn't want to tell you, but I saw a strange look in his eyes Friday night. He was off to himself in the bushes behind the store. I went to the restroom and when I came out, our eyes met. He suddenly just looked away. It was a kind of uncomfortable moment. Maybe I should have told you. I just figured he might have had a little too much to drink."

We approached the house where Rex and I had played as children. It hadn't been updated much since then. "Let me go see what's going on," I said, leaving her in the truck with Goose.

I knocked on the screen door, and when I got no response, I pushed it open gently as it squeaked on its hinges. "Rex," I called. I walked back to his bedroom.

Rex was sitting on the floor beside the old iron bed in his room. He sat there on the wide-plank wood floor and barely lifted his head when I came in. He looked up at me with tiny pupils in his dark eyes. His hands were shaking uncontrollably.

"I screwed up, man," he said, hanging his head. I went to the hall bathroom and wet a wash cloth and took it to him to put on his throat. It might keep the nausea at bay and keep him awake. "I really screwed up."

"It's okay. Let's get you to an emergency room before you pass out. I'm not asking questions right now. We'll talk more later." He nodded his head and reached for my hand.

We walked out, and he got in the truck, pushing Lora to the middle slot in the bench seat. I must have given her a look that conveyed what was happening because she didn't say a word. She just put her arm around Rex's shoulders as we drove down the mountain into the nearest town that would have an emergency clinic or hospital.

Guess I should have called Mrs. Jolie, but I didn't know what I'd tell her. I knew she was worried about him from the look she gave me back at the store. I'll call her after we get him checked out and tell her what's going on.

Rex spent the night in the hospital. I took Lora home and went back and slept on the hard plastic pull-out chair-bed in his room. Sleep never did really come. Between fighting the sheets, slipping on the plastic seat covers, and listening to voices in my head, I doubt I ever really closed my eyes. After they checked him in the ER, the doctor recommended that he spend the night for some tests.

"He nearly overdosed," the doctor had told me and asked some questions about his history with drugs. I told him I thought Rex had been clean for about a year.

"Maybe so, but if he had not been using and went back to the same dosage he was taking when he quit, it could have been fatal. Glad you found him. I'll make some recommendations on rehab and a mentor program before he is released. We just need to get him flushed out and give him something to fight the withdrawals."

I looked over at him in the bed, circles under his eyes and noticed for the first time that he was thinner than he should have been. He had been clean about a year. How had this happened again without my noticing? I never saw it coming.

He opened his eyes and looked at me with an embarrassed and somewhat panicky look. His hands shook as he pulled the sheet up to his chin.

"Did you call mama?" he asked.

"Yeah, I told her you weren't feeling good, maybe dehydrated from a bug or something. We will have to tell her the real deal soon."

He turned his head to stare at the wall.

"What's going on, Man?" I asked. He was silent for a few minutes.

"It never goes away, you know. Working at the store has been great. Hanging out with you guys on Fridays has saved my life. Sometimes it's just stronger than I am."

"Let's do some straight talking to the doc and see what he recommends," I said.

He was quiet but didn't argue. The nurse came in and put something in his I-V and left. Rex took a deep breath and seemed to drift off to sleep.

I looked at my watch—7 a.m. I could still make it to school on time. I stopped by the nurses' station and left my name and number and told them I'd be back later to check on him. The head nurse didn't know if he would be released today or not. I'd have to call Mrs. Jolie when I had a break at school. I dreaded it like the plague.

"Hey, Mrs. Jolie," I said when she answered the phone. "Rex is down at a small hospital about 20 minutes from here."

"What in the world is wrong, Sam?" she asked. I could hear the worry in her voice.

"I am afraid he fell off the wagon," I told her. I heard a sharp intake of her breath. "I know he has struggled to do good this past year, but I think the doctor will probably recommend another trip to rehab."

"Oh, dear. I thought he was getting in trouble again." She said she would get one of the workers at the station across the road to drive her over to stay with him for the day.

"What about the store?" I asked.

"I'll just shut the damn doors and put a 'Be Right Back' sign up."

We hung up and I took time to call Lora and had basically the same conversation. "I need to go back over tonight," I told her.

"Do you want me to go with you?" she asked. "He might talk to you better if I'm not around."

"Well, I'd sure like your company, but you may be right. How about I stop by and see you after I leave the hospital? Is that too late?"

"Not at all," she said.

I thought about Lora the rest of the day at school. When I think about her, I get a warm spot in my heart. Guess I'll have to do something about that. I never knew what my life was missing until I found it.

Chapter 19
Lora • 1997 • West Virginia

Sam has gone back to the hospital to check on Rex. I could hear the worry in his voice when he called after school today. He's missing his afternoon art lessons, and I know he never likes to do that. Come to think about it, I'm beginning to know a lot about Sam Woods.

He offers himself up with no pretense. He wears what he wants without a thought as to whether it's in style or not. At school, he has taken initiatives with his students like taking them on field trips and teaching outside the four walls of a classroom. No other teacher at that school has done that.

Today I am going up in the mountains to visit with an older gentleman who makes mountain dulcimers.

This man is the go-to person in the mountains for a hand-made dulcimer. Rod Swanson lives in a beautiful cabin high in Appalachia. He was expecting me this morning when I drove Mrs. Wilmer's car up the hairpin curves to his house and shop.

I'm going to have to do something about a car or truck. I can't keep borrowing her vehicle. When I put gas in it, I feel guilty even though she insists that it needs driving.

It will be really hard for me to get around before long as winter nears. Even the local people even find it difficult to drive these mountain roads if there is snow and ice, and they have chains on their tires. I hear it's not uncommon to get stranded somewhere and have to wait it out.

Rod Swanson opened the door of his workshop for me before I reached the front steps. I could tell the minute I saw him that I'd like him. I told him about the research I was doing, and he seemed truly fascinated. He may have asked me more about music in Mississippi than I did

about music in West Virginia. Rod is a tall but stocky man, slightly stooped in his 70th year. He has a neatly-trimmed beard and wears his graying hair combed back.

He dresses in jeans and a worn flannel shirt most of the time. You can see brown marks on his hands where the wood stains have seeped into the cracks in his dried craftsman's fingers.

"I don't know where to start, Mr. Swanson," I said, taking in every detail of his workshop. There was ordered chaos there. Various woods were stacked on metal shelving. That shop also held tools, glues, stains, clamps, drawn patterns and other tools of his trade. Swanson sat on a well-worn workman's stool with curled wood shavings of different colors under his feet. His brown and stained apron was draped over the back.

"Just tell me what you want to know, young lady," he said.

"Why don't you just talk, and I'll listen. Start with how you learned your craft and then tell me details on what makes your instruments special."

"To start with, my actual title is a luthier. That's someone who makes or repairs stringed instruments that have a box and a neck. There are two kinds of luthiers, really. Some make instruments that are meant to be played with a bow. Then there are those like me, who make instruments that are meant to be plucked or strummed."

He went on to tell me about how he chooses different woods to get the perfect tone, one that will give the dulcimer its richness and warmth. "I use walnut to get a rich mellow sound," said Mr. Swanson. "Cherry and mahogany have a brighter sound. They are both beautiful, just depends on what you like."

He went on to pick a few tunes for me that made me smile. "Mountain music takes its time," he said, plucking out an old standard hymn in the traditional style and then speeding up to show me the Bluegrass or mountain style which was higher and used many more notes.

I couldn't help but think about Sam as he goes through a similar selection process for woods in his carvings.

"You think I could learn to do that?" I asked with excitement in my voice.

"Sure you can. Come sit by me and put your feet on that stool so that your knees are flat. Helps you keep your instrument on your lap, and it's easier to play." He showed me where to put my fingers of my left hand and where to place my right hand on the dulcimer. You can use a little wooden stick tool or a pick, larger than a guitar pick. With his guidance, I actually played a few chords.

We must have talked and played longer than I'd thought. I looked up and noticed the winter sun falling making a purple and orange glow in the sky.

"Mr. Swanson, I must go," I told him. "I've enjoyed our talk so much that I let the time get away from me. I hope you don't mind if I call you back if I have more questions."

"Not at all," he said as he escorted me to the door. We said goodbye, and I started my trip down the mountain.

I secretly hoped that when I got back to Helen's that Sam would call me with good news about Rex and invite me to his cabin.

Hardly had I time to get back to Helen's and

change clothes before Sam called, inviting me to the cabin.

"Is it too late for you to come up here and eat a nice fish dinner?" he asked. "I'll tell you about Rex," he added.

"No, it's fine. But can you come get me? I don't have the heart to ask Helen to let me take her car again. Plus, I'm still not too good navigating these mountain roads in the winter, especially at night."

"Sure," he said, with a hint of excitement in his voice. "I'll be right there. We can cook when we get here."

We pulled up at Sam's cabin about a half hour later. It really is a beautiful and peaceful place. The winter sun was just setting and casting a beautiful orange glow on the water.

"Come on in. I'll start the fish. Do you want to make a salad? The lettuce and fixins' are in the refrigerator."

He seemed to know his way around his small kitchen. I turned to get the vegetables from the fridge and something on the deck caught my eye. I stared with amazement.

I saw from the back what looked like a near-life size carving of a woman with her arm draped around a dog that looked remarkably like Goose. The woman looked like me. The drapes in the woman's shawl were executed perfectly. And I knew the dog was Goose because the wooden dog's tail had a crook in it near the end. Goose's tail had gotten caught in the truck door when he was a pup and was never completely straight again.

I looked up at Sam. He smiled. "Are you offended that I carved you without your knowing?"

"Offended? I'm honored. Did you ask Goose?" He smiled and pulled me to him and we shared our first deep kiss.

"Dinner is going to be great," he said, pushing a loose strand of hair away from my face. "But breakfast is going to be even better. You staying?"

I stepped back into his arms. "You bet."

Sam looked up as I walked out of the cabin bedroom rubbing sleep from my eyes. I was wearing the long sleeve T-shirt I had on last night and socks. My hair had escaped from its braid and fell to my shoulders.

"Morning, beautiful," he said with a mischievous smile as he flipped a huge pancake on the stove griddle.

"Now, don't start that stuff," I said as I worked out the tangles in my hair and let it hang loose around my shoulders. I hugged him from behind. He turned and returned the hug and nuzzled my neck.

When I looked up, he was smiling. "I'm glad you stayed," he said.

"Me too. So what's for breakfast?" I asked looking over the pile of mixing bowls, egg shells, and bacon scattered on the small counter.

"Pancakes and bacon! My specialty. In fact, it's the only non-grill thing I can do, except for peanut butter sandwiches."

Goose was sitting on the deck looking in the screen door. His tail was thumping so hard I thought it might break. He was licking his lips and moving his front feet back and forth.

Sam looked at him and smiled. "At least I'll have one customer," he said.

"You'll have two," I answered. "What can I do?"

"Just sit there on that stool and look pretty

and try not to look at Goose. It only makes it worse."

What a way to start the morning! If they could all be this great. I'm afraid to wish they could.

Chapter 20
Simsie • 1998 • Mississippi

Christmas came and went. We celebrated here with a few friends. I know Buck was missing Mr. Asa something terrible. We even drove over to spend a day or two with my mother and brother. They really liked Buck, and that was a huge relief to me.

Out little church in Mississippi looked so beautiful at Christmas. The red candles in the window made a sweet glow as we walked up the sidewalk for Christmas Eve services. This time last year I never dreamed I'd be here, in this church, holding the hand of this tall, beautiful, blonde man. Prayers were answered.

We are having a February wedding. I'm so excited, and so is Buck. The other day Lora called to say that she thought we should live permanently in Mr. Asa's house. Buck is already there. What will we do if she decides to come back home? Guess we can work all that out when the time comes, but for now it will be home for us.

The wedding is not far away. Lora is coming home and bringing her friend Sam with her. My mother and brother are going to be here. People from the church will come. It will be small, simple, and beautiful.

I was cleaning up in the farmhouse this week and saw another carved "V." This one was in the kitchen pantry. It's just a small area off the kitchen that has an old curtain for a door. There inside the shelves was the letter. The last time I told Lora about seeing one on the post near where Sister got hurt, it seemed to upset her.

I can't figure out who could have made these marks. We are the only ones here, and when we leave, we lock the doors. When I ask Buck, he doesn't seem too concerned about it.

"Probably made by a kid long ago," he said.

I don't think that's right. Because I've been in this house for a while now, and I've never seen this before.

When March comes, I may change jobs. I've applied to work at a minor medical clinic about twenty minutes away. There's a pretty good chance that I'll get it. The pay will be better there. We will be fine. Lora pays Buck for his work, and he gets a percentage of the cow sales.

We haven't had another strange encounter with Ben Hubbard. Sister has almost healed completely. If you know her like Buck and I do, you can tell she has a slight limp when she really turns it on to go after a cow. When she was hurt, we let her come into the kitchen to sleep. Buck says she is still sleeping there.

We filed a report with the local Sheriff's Office after Sister's shooting but haven't heard anything. We have no proof who shot her, no eye witness. I guess there is not much they can do.

My brother is coming from Tennessee a few days early to help me move things from my apartment to the farm house. I don't have much.

For now, I'll just be happy living in the old farmhouse with Buck. It needs some repairs that we can probably make ourselves. I don't think it's a good idea for me to start redecorating and changing things up. That would upset Buck since he sometimes doesn't do too good with change. We have plenty of time for that later.

Since our talk in the cemetery that day about his mama, I've done a little research. It seems she is living in Tennessee, up near Memphis. I can't believe she has been this close all this time and never had a real part in Buck's life. That must hurt more than he is able to tell me.

Her name now is Paulette T. Greer, so she must have married at some point. A newspaper clipping I found on microfiche in the library shows her with a daughter and baby at the grand opening of her flower shop in Tennessee, close to where she lives now.

I still think we should call her and invite her to the wedding. If she doesn't want to come, at least we made the effort. Maybe I can talk to Buck about it this afternoon. I can just see his face now. He will pout.

I did talk to him, and he flatly refused to call her. "Why don't you call her, Simsie?" he said, looking a little put out with me.

"I think that should be your place Buck, but if you want her to come at all, I will. He just nodded and left the room.

After several failed attempts, I finally found her phone number. This will be awkward I know, but I'll give it a try. I dialed the number and waited.

"Hello," said a somewhat shaky female voice.

"Mrs. Greer?"

"Yes, who is this?" she asked skeptically.

"You don't know me. My name is Mary Simmons Montgomery. Please don't hang up. I'm engaged to your son, John."

There was silence. Finally, she said, "Yes?"

"We are planning on getting married in February, and I'd like to send you an invitation to the wedding if you would like to come."

There was more silence. "Does John want me to come?" she asked. "We haven't really been in touch."

"If you would be comfortable coming, we'd love for you to be a part of the wedding."

Silence.

"If you want to send me an invitation, I'll think about it. Not sure I'll come. Tell John he has a half-sister he might want to meet." She gave me her address, thanked me, and hung up.

I thought about this for a while before talking to Buck. Why had she left him when he was so young? Who was his daddy? From the few photos Buck has of her, I couldn't see much resemblance. Buck did have her blonde hair color, but that was about it.

She was a nice-looking young woman, but sad. Her clothes let you know that she didn't have much and had worked hard all her life. There were so many unanswered questions.

Buck had pushed all that back since he was five. Maybe he wasn't ready to see her after all these years. Maybe the wedding was not the right place for a reunion. We have a lot to think about. Right now, I'm just going to leave him alone. It's almost suppertime, and that usually cheers him up.

When I found him outside, he was sitting on

the porch step with his elbows resting on his knees, feet wide apart. He was staring at the ground but not seeing anything. He looked up when the screen door opened.

"Did you find her?" he asked with a hurtful look in his voice. "What did she say? How did she sound? Is she coming?"

"Hold on, Buck. I did talk to her. She said to send her an invitation and she would think about it. She didn't say, 'No.'"

He looked back at the ground. "She won't come," he said, in a small boy's voice.

"I did find out that you have a sister and a baby nephew. Let's just wait and see what happens. Want to come in for supper?"

"I'll be there in a minute. I just want to sit here a while," he said.

I left him there on the porch steps with his thoughts, his hurts, and his hopes.

Chapter 21
Buck • 1998 • Mississippi

The closer the wedding gets, the more scared I am—not about marrying Simsie. I can't believe God has blessed me with this woman who loves me. I never dreamed I'd find this happiness.

What I dread is this business about my mama coming to the wedding. If she comes, what will I say? How will she look? What will she think of me? The last time I saw her I was a teenager. She drove over and we had lunch at a little cafe in town.

It was hard to talk to her. What do you say

to someone you barely know? She was nice enough, but quiet, like she didn't know me at all. Guess she doesn't.

I've tried to justify her leaving me on that porch so many years ago. I guess I'll never understand how she could leave her kid. Simsie and I have talked about having a kid or two. I'd be the best daddy I could. Since I didn't have a daddy, the only role model I had was Mr. Asa. He was better to me than most dads are to their own kids.

If my mama comes, it might put a damper on our day. If she doesn't come, it will hurt, like it has all my life. Looks like a no-win situation to me. Simsie says I have a sister. She may not even know about me. Wonder what she's like? I don't know what to think about all this. Besides all this family stuff, I'm so excited about having Simsie here with me all the time.

January is a hard time for us here on the farm. I've been looking back at Mr. Asa's little black calendar book that came from the feed store. He kept real good records. In that book he wrote when calves were born, when cattle were wormed or doctored, when to vaccinate and other details about the livestock.

I guess now is a good time to start that my-self—it being the first of the year. We always liked winter calves. If the weather is too bad or below freezing, it can be a problem. But summer calves suffer in the heat and with the flies. Wonder what Simsie will do the first time I bring a calf in the kitchen for her to bottle fed. You have to do that if you lose the mama or if the calf is born and stays wet with temperatures dropping. I imagine she will be a good calf nurse.

We have about 50 cows ready to calve. This time of year, I check cows in the truck instead of horseback. Unless one comes up missing, then I have to saddle up and go find it. Times like these are when I really need Sister. She should be up to working now that she has had some time off.

Mr. Asa wrote other things in his little book. He kept up with doctor visits and when he got a haircut. And he wrote about Lora. He wrote down every time she called or when he called her. I know he missed her. He loved her enough to let her be her own person, but that didn't fill the hole she left when she moved around after college.

That little book was sort of a diary for him. He also wrote about his sweet wife, Lora's mother. Mr. Asa never had another lady friend, that I know of, after his wife died. He just settled in here at the farm and enjoyed life with Lora and, I hope, with me. Then I saw this note he wrote about a month before he died.

"Buckshot is turning into a real hand. I watch him working cows and horses and keeping up with the equipment. I think a few of my ways may have rubbed off on him. That little Simsie has been a gift for him. Wouldn't hurt my feelings if they moved in here and had a few kids of their own. Might be the only way I get 'grandkids.'"

Chapter 22
Lora • 1998 • West Virginia

It's been two months since my first night with Sam at his cabin. After that night, I backed off and went to work on my project. I needed some time to think about what was happening. And something was definitely happening.

We talked every other day or so. I went with him to a couple of Friday night pickin's. This time of year it is so cold up here that we just had to gather around the stove in Mrs. Jolie's store. It was kind of sad since Rex was not there. He has spent the last six weeks in a new rehab center.

Different doctors, different type of therapy. So far, so good, according to Sam. He has been such a loyal friend, making the 50-mile one-way trek to see him every Sunday. I went with him once, but stayed in the lobby and read while they visited. I knew they needed time alone.

Sometimes Sam brought him magazines and books. Rex got to go outside on one particularly sunny day, and he and Sam walked around the beautiful campus. Rock outcroppings provided natural seats for patients and families to take in the mountain views. A barely-visible fence around the property ensured safety for the patients.

"Rex is coming around," Sam told me. "I think he may need more to occupy his time than just running the store. He feels guilty about not being there for his mama, but needs to do something else. I've about talked him into going back to college. He only went one semester before the habit got him, and he dropped out.

"I think I can find some kids from school who would jump at the chance to help at the store in the afternoons. Now is not the time to make big decisions, but at least he is thinking about making his life better.

"My life is better with you in it," he said, smiling at me across the truck seat.

I nodded and smiled back. This relationship has been near perfect so far. I'm afraid if I go farther, I'll get hurt.

There's something I haven't told Sam. I'm still thinking about possibilities before I say anything. Last week when I checked my mail at Helen's I found a card notifying me to come to the post office to sign for a piece of registered mail. I couldn't imagine what it was. It couldn't be good.

I walked to the little Post Office in town and showed my card to the lady at the window. She smiled and returned with a legal size envelope. I took it with me and sat down on the little bench near the sidewalk.

It was such a beautiful day that I hated to open that letter and ruin it. The letter was from the agency that hired me to do the mountain research.

Dear Ms. Sinclair:

I regret to inform you that the private funding for the West Virginia/Southern States project has ended. We will no longer require your services on this project. You can expect a prorated payment for your work up to this point. Please send an itemized and documented report to show your expenses to date. The information you have gathered and may continue to gather will be solely your own. We will claim no rights to your findings. We are sorry this culturally-relevant project has ended.

Sincerely,

Davis McGee

Project Administrator

Well. That is enough to make your head spin. I can't say I'm especially sorry. In doing my research, I found that these customs have been over-documented. The mountain culture had not been compared to those in the Southern states, and that's what got my attention in the first place.

I have gathered enough information and

photographs to pitch a series of articles to regional publications in the South or in the mountains. I don't think the time spent here has been wasted.

I'm not telling Sam yet, or Helen. I think I'll stay here a while longer to see where this relationship is going. I am beginning to love waking up to the blue mist of the mountains.

So for now, my mouth is zipped.

I walked back to my room at Helen's and dialed Sam's number. He answered on the third ring, just as I was about to hang up.

"Are you in the middle of a lesson?" I asked.

"No, just finishing up. What's on your mind?"

"How about I get some steaks and come up there and you cook them for me?" I waited.

"Why don't I come get you and the steaks?"

"That's even better."

We hung up, and as I walked over to look in the wardrobe for something comfortable to wear, I caught a glimpse of myself in the antique mirror on Helen's little dresser. I was humming an unknown melody and looked right proud of myself.

Sam picked me up, and we began our climb up the mountain to his cabin. "How's your project coming?" Sam asked, giving me a serious look.

"Oh, pretty good," I said, hoping to change the subject.

"How was the dulcimer maker?"

"Really nice. He does good work."

"Are you quiet for some reason tonight?" he asked, reaching across the back of the truck seat to rest his hand on my shoulder.

"No, not really. You talk to me. Talk to me about Rex, about your after school classes, about your students in school. Just talk." I reached to take his hand, and Goose, who was planted firmly between us, caught my hand and flipped it over on his head for a pat.

"So much for romance with you around, Goose," I said, laughing softly.

I listened to his beautiful deep voice, that I had grown accustomed to, as he described his day's events. The music of his mountain accent combined with the rumble of the old truck, lulled me into a perfectly-calm state. By the time we got to his place, all was good.

After grilling steaks on the deck, we settled into an old wooden swing and wrapped up in his truck quilt as we listened to the sounds of the lake.

"You really fit in here pretty good, Lora," he said with a huskiness in his voice. "Do you think we have something here?" His brown eyes searched mine.

"I'd like to think we do. I just don't need to be hurt. My track record isn't too great."

"I won't hurt you, if that's what you are worried about. I've waited a long time for someone like you to come along."

I felt myself sink into the circle of his arms. "I want you to come to Mississippi with me for Buck's wedding. See where I come from. Then we'll talk more. For now, I'm getting used to this, too."

"I'd be honored to go to the wedding," he said. "If you give me an idea what they might like, I can do a carving for a wedding present. What do you think?"

"The chocolate lab carving was so beautiful. What if I get you a photo of Sister and you do a carving of her in her Border Collie crouch?"

"Perfect," he said. "Can't wait."

We just sat there watching the moon over the lake, listening to the water lap onto the ground at the foot of the deck. He would tell I was getting sleepy. "Better take you back," he said. "I don't want to, but it's a school night."

"You sound like Asa," I said smiling.

Chapter 23
Lora • 1998 • West Virginia

I woke up this morning looking out my window at Helen's at the beautiful morning mist. I was falling in love with these mountains. Did that mean that I was disloyal to my Mississippi? After grabbing a pair of old jeans and a t-shirt, I went downstairs, being careful to walk softly in case the old stairs creaked. I thought Helen might still be asleep.

She was not. I found her already dressed and drinking coffee at the kitchen table with a book in her hand. "Hey Lora," she said as I crept into the kitchen. "Coffee is ready."

"Oh, Helen, I was afraid I'd wake you. I woke up early and couldn't go back to sleep. Coffee is what I need."

"I'm going up to the cabin to clean up a little and check on the pipes. Would you want to ride up there with me?" Helen offered. "Some of the roads might be a little patchy in the shade, but I think we will be okay."

"Oh, that would be great," I said. "I really didn't have any plans for the day."

"Good. After we have our coffee, we will head on up there. I still need to get a few cleaning supplies. We aren't in a hurry. Maybe the sun will warm some of the icy patches."

We had become comfortable enough with each other that we could sit in silence, drinking our coffee, reading or watching the morning news . That's a nice feeling.

After a relaxing half hour, I went upstairs to braid my hair and grab a coat and gloves. In the mountains, you always have to be prepared. Helen always keeps a blanket, coat, gloves, and a flashlight in a box in her car, just in case.

We started the drive up the mountain. I noticed she was driving in the direction of Sam's cabin. "Is your cabin close to Sam's?" I asked.

"Same direction, but I doubt you'd find it if you didn't know where to look."

She gripped the steering wheel with both hands, a little nervous driving on the roads with patches of snow and ice. We passed Sam's place and finally turned off on a small path, not gravel, just packed dirt covered in pine straw. After winding around a few turns, I saw the place, perched high on the mountain, overlooking a lake.

"Oh Helen, this is breathtaking," I said. "I bet if you were here during a big snow you just had to stay put."

"You've got that right. If we even thought we might get stranded, we left the cars closer to the road and drove the four-wheeler in and out." I got a mental picture of Helen riding with her arms around Steve, her hair blowing in the wind. That kind of joy had seeped from her face.

We got out of the car, collecting the bag of cleaning supplies, and started up the outdoor set of stairs. Pushing the huge wooden door open, I stepped inside and just looked with wonder. Helen was smiling when she saw my reaction.

Stepping in the front door we landed on a hand-hooked spirit rug. I looked up. The ceiling over the fireplace must have reached 20 feet high. Most of the back of the living area was comprised of windows, looking over the water and at the mountains. Rough beams braced the ceiling. Hanging from the beam near the kitchen area was an intricately-woven tribal rug in orange, yellow, tan, and rust colors.

Pottery lined the open shelves in the kitchen and was showcased on the mantel, which was also a rough-cut beam.

There was one large bedroom and bath off the kitchen area. Instead of lodge pole furniture that you might expect in a log home, Helen and Steve had a huge burled walnut plantation bed. The headboard, with its intricate carving, was over six feet tall. On the bed was a vintage log cabin-patterned quilt in fall colors of green, rusty orange, gold and red. There was a primitive blanket chest at the footboard. The dresser and chest looked like they came from the same period, about 1880. Both had white marble tops.

Outside the bedroom was an antique highboy bookcase and secretary. The wood was a rich mahogany. Filling the bookcases were beautifully-bound classic books, Moby Dick, Tales of Poe, The Last of the Mohicans, Mary Shelley's Frankenstein, works by Charles Dickens and more. The colors of the spines seemed to mimic those found in the quilt.

Mixed in with the books were antique paperweights, little framed watercolors, and a bronze statuette of a golden retriever.

Another small room that now served as an office and library was on the other side of the kitchen. It could also be a bedroom, I guess. It held a massive, more masculine desk, exposed brick fireplace and mantel and bookshelves filled with more modern books, beautifully-framed photographs and other pieces of art and antiques that Steve and Helen had collected over the years.

I turned to Helen, my mouth must have been open wide enough for a bird to fly in. She gave me a sweet and sad smile. "Oh Helen, I'm at a loss for words. How do you ever leave this place?"

"Leaving is not the hard part, coming back is. I hear Steve in every creak of the floor board,

I see him hanging the rug, placing the stones in the fireplace. We loved to go to little out-of-the- way shops and collect books and other treasures."

"Let's sit down," I suggested, leading her over to the leather sofa. When I sat down, I took her hand. "You didn't come here to clean, did you?"

"Well, I do see a little dust here and there. I really just wanted you to see it, so you would understand my sadness. Sometimes I know I'm not good company. I'm so grateful to have had those years with him and to have my daughter and granddaughter, but I miss him so much."

When I pressed her hand, she sighed and fought back the tears that were burning her eyes. "What if you came up here more often, like for a weekend? Would it help if I came with you?"

"I hadn't thought of that," she admitted. "Maybe we will try it soon, in the spring, if you are still here."

"You know I have a feeling I will be." We sat in silence as we watched the sun reflecting off the lake, and the hawks flying over hoping to catch a small varmint.

"I think I'll make us another cup of coffee."

I couldn't wait to tell Sam about the cabin. I didn't want to make him feel like his was dingy in comparison. It was great, beautiful views, but it did look like a man and a Goose lived there. That thought made me feel happy inside.

Chapter 24
Simsie • 1998 • Mississippi

The days for the wedding are coming so fast. I'm getting used to the idea of being a farmer's wife. As much as I like the idea of having my own independence, I want to be part of a family, too. My nursing job gives us an income, so I won't have to worry so much about what the farm makes.

I grew up in a house where my parents worked office jobs. I never dreamed I'd sit in the kitchen of an old farmhouse with a baby calf wrapped in one of my blankets giving it a bottle. Buck said we might have to do that if a calf was in trouble. He must have been testing me to see how I'd react. I think he was surprised when my eyes lit up at the idea.

I felt so proud when we got that baby healthy enough to get up on its spindly legs and walk. After a few days of special care, we guided her out the back screen porch, down the steps and into the lot where her mama was calling her.

My eyes met Buck's. We were both smiling. What's a little dirt on the kitchen floor? I like the old screened-in back porch. It was built onto the house in the 50s. It's a good place to stomp off the mud on the back stone steps and kick off your boots on the porch. There's always a boot jack near the door to pry the boot right off your tired feet.

This porch is where Mr. Asa's mother used to do the laundry. They never moved the old wringer washer. More than laundry has been washed in the big concrete sink.

It has probably held a puppy, a watermelon, a mess of butterbeans, and maybe even a baby or two.

I like to ride around and look at the beautiful homes downtown. Those homes are so pretty, but they wouldn't stand a chance out here in the country where we work hard and get dirty.

Shelves on the back porch held vintage canning jars. They must have been used over and over to put up Mrs. Lydia's vegetables. They sat there reflecting light on the floor of the porch. I don't know if I'm up to canning. Maybe I'll give it a try. I'll have to learn about gardening. The old garden spot has been barren since Buck was a little boy. Seems strange when you can get all the canned green beans and tomatoes you want at grocery stores in town. Buck says the home-canned ones are better.

I'm sure those shelves would be prettier with jars of pickles, tomatoes, green beans, and jellies all lined up in a row. We'd have to find a place for that in the pantry, so the food and the jars won't freeze or get too hot.

The house is more modern now than it was during Mrs. Lydia's time. But much of the past is still there to see. I'll never know the people who lived here except through their possessions which reflect how they lived. I regret that I didn't get to know Mr. Asa better. I can see his ways in Buck, and Lora. too, the little I've been with her.

I watch Buck saddling his horse, taking his

time. I like that. Since I do know a little about horses, I respect a man who is good to his horse. I've got nothing for these guys who hot rod around on their horses, jerking on their heads, getting in their mouths, getting them all stirred up.

Buck approaches his horse like he does everything else, with kindness. At the end of the day, Checker, a big line-back dun, gets a nice pat on the rump. No fuss. Just thanks for a job well done. He washes him off when it's warm enough, never puts him up dirty—takes care of his horse and his tack.

When I ride with Buck, he puts me on "Runaway" Rose. We laugh at her name because she probably couldn't run away if she tried. She's way too fat. Maybe I can ride her more and put her on a diet.

I sit at the dining room table and watch Buck out the back window as he talks quietly to Checker while he goes through this end-of-the-day routine. I smile when Buck shakes the hair back from his face.

Buck's long, tanned fingers look like they belong to a working man. At the end of the day, that's not dirt under his fingernails, but stains left by horse sweat, fence mending, tractor repair, and all the jobs that cross his path in his workday. When he tries, he cleans up remarkably well.

Sister lies in front of the barn in the shade watching his every move. She must have gone with him because she is panting. I can tell from here that she has a few beggar lice for me to comb out after supper. I can see that, by living this life, I'll never be bored. We can have a mix of old ways and new and find our own way of life here on this farm.

Chapter 25
Lora • 1998 • Mississippi
Part III-The Wedding

Last night at Sam's, after a nice dinner of fish, baked potatoes and West Virginia cole-slaw, I asked him again if he was sure he wanted to go with me to Mississippi to Buck's wedding.

"What's wrong with you, girl?" he joked. "I've already told you my bags are packed." He reached over and pretended to knock me on the head.

Smiling at his playfulness I said, "Just making sure. I will order our plane tickets tomorrow. Can you get a sub at school? The wedding is on Saturday, so I need to go Wednesday to help Simsie get ready. We could come home Sunday. Is that a problem?"

"Nope. What do I need to wear? I have a sports coat but that's about it. I'll try not to embarrass you."

"Never," I said, leaning over for a kiss. "Small country church. That should be fine."

I felt any reservations I'd had about a relationship with this man fading day by day.

Wednesday is a week from today. I'd better get busy.

Tickets are purchased, bags are packed, and we are ready to go. Rex is out of rehab now and doing well. Sam asked him to come and check on Goose to make sure he had food and doesn't run off thinking we were gone forever.

Arrangements have been made for Sam's classes, and he cancelled his afternoon art classes for a few days.

I found a vintage-looking light rose-colored dress that comes to just above my ankles. I think it will be perfect for a wedding in a little country church. Sam will be handsome in whatever he wears—slacks, sports jacket, boots, his brown curls touching the neck of his collar.

We boarded our plane and had plenty of time on our five-hour flight for some good conversation. Sam asked me a million questions about Buck and our family. Most of the questions about Buck were hard for me to answer. I barely remember his mother and don't know anything about her background.

"Buck says his mother might come to the wedding," I added. "I can't tell if he is happy or worried about that." Sam nodded.

Before we had left West Virginia, I found Sam in his woodworking shop one afternoon. He jumped when he saw me come in.

"I wasn't ready for you to see this," he responded to my startled look. "Oh, okay," he said, carefully unwrapping tissue paper from an object he was placing in a wooden box. It was the carving of Sister.

I smiled and felt tears burning my eyes at the same time. It was perfect from the tip of her little black nose to the end of her fluffy white tail. He had captured her in a typical Border Collie crouch, her eyes intent on whatever livestock she was herding.

"Oh, Sam, they will love it. Her markings are exactly right. Thank you so much for doing this for them."

"It will be from both of us," he said. "Your idea, my wood." I loved him hard at that exact moment.

The little wooden box was in a sack that he had stowed underneath his plane seat. I looked down and smiled. He winked back.

We will be arriving in Memphis in about thirty minutes. I'm not sure who is meeting us. Buck said he would take care of it. He is probably busy with last-minute details.

Simsie's mother and brother are coming also today to help her with decorating the church for the wedding and reception.

I can't wait to see them, to be back in Mississippi, to see it through Sam's eyes. His reaction to my home will let me know where this relationship might be going.

Chapter 26
Lora • 1998 • Mississippi

We are finally home. Simsie picked us up at the airport in Memphis this morning. This particular homecoming was special with Sam at my side. I saw everything from his point of view—from the old farmhouse and barn, to the land that was so different from the scenery of West Virginia. Buck has done a great job of keeping the operation running by himself but that left little time for maintenance and repairs.

Sam is the kind of guy who puts people at ease. He immediately established a friendship with Buck and Simsie.

When he met Sister, he knelt on one knee and looked her right in the eye. She held his gaze, but her tail was thumping on the hard dirt the whole time. Sister's approval speaks loud to Buck and me. Buck just smiled at me over Sam's head as we watched the two get to know each other.

If it weren't winter and so cold, Sam would like nothing better than for Buck to take him fishing in the big pond behind the barn. They could sit on the levee and feel the breeze that usually stirs across the pond. I'm sure Buck would be telling all about his favorite stories of growing up here on the place—about working hard since he was eight, about the time he got lost when he stayed out too late in the woods hunting, and about finding Simsie. I hope he doesn't tell him too many stories about me. That could get me in trouble.

Tomorrow morning, I will go to the church and help decorate the tables. Sam and I will go gather greenery from what used to be the old orchard next to the corn crib. Light snow is predicted.

Tonight Simsie and Buck are at a small

rehearsal dinner given by the ladies of the church. It will be such a small wedding a rehearsal is not really needed. It is just a time of celebration and fellowship.

I stand at the dining room window looking out over the West pasture. Sunsets are magnificent no matter where in the world, but I tend to believe the sunsets from this particular window are the most stunning. The trees at the edge of the pasture are silhouetted black against a bright orange sky bordered by streaks of purple and pink. I exhale.

Sam walks up behind me quietly. "Look," I point in the direction of the pasture. "I have no words for this except that when I see this I know I'm home."

We turned from the window for just a minute, and when we looked back, the orange had faded.

As I walk around the house, Sam follows me as I look at our family treasures through his eyes. "Those are my grandparents," I point at a black and white photo in a carved wooden frame. "Mama and Daddy on their wedding day," I say as I give him a tour in the hall of the house, the original dog trot porch. "That's me and Star," I smile as he looks at me at age of 6, wearing cowboy boots with my school dress as I try to climb up on the wooly pony.

I hear Sam chuckle. "Wild child," he teases. "Are there pictures of Buck?" I take him back to Buck's room where we find photos of Buck fishing, Buck and me with the cow dogs of the day, Buck and Daddy on the tractor, and a small framed picture of Paulette on his bedside table. Our eyes met with a look of sadness.

Sam ran his fingers over the crooked walking stick that had belonged to my great-granddaddy and checked out the set of cow horns covered with rust velvet that hung over the bedroom door.

"Let's give them the present when they get back," I suggest. Sam nods.

"Are we sleeping in your old room"

"I guess so, but if Daddy was still here, you would be on that hard couch."

Finally, as we nearly drifted off to sleep in front of the fire in Daddy's room, Buck and

Simsie tumble into the room, full of excitement, their faces flushed from the cold. He
couldn't wait to tell us all about the dinner,
while Simsie showed us more gifts they had
gotten afterward.

There was something endearing about the
innocence of their love. They seemed grateful
for even the small gestures of kindness shown
them.

"We have a little something for you, too," I
said, holding Sam's hand. He went back to
my room and returned with the small wooden
box.

"Pardon our lack of gift wrapping," Sam said,
offering the box to Buck. Simsie, at his elbow,
looked on with anticipation as he opened the
box and removed the blue velvet fabric that
covered the carving.

Buck turned the carving of Sister over and
over in his hands, finally handing it to Simsie.
"Where did you get it? Who did it," he asked,
full of questions.

We saw them as their eyes met. "It's from
both of us," explained Sam. "It was Lora's idea,
and my wood."

"How did you do this?" asked Buck, his face

showing his complete awe that someone could take a piece of wood and find a perfect Sister inside it.

"I carve," said Sam.

"Well what do you think?" I asked Sam as we made our way out in the cold to the orchard. "Is it too early to tell?"

"Well, I can certainly see how you would love this land," he said, linking his arm in mine. I had carried a basket to collect leaves and berries. "Do you think Buck can keep the place up?"

"I think so," I said. "Simsie is a good fit for him. She can help in ways where he isn't so good, like the book work, record keeping, ordering supplies, that kind of thing. Nobody has the working knowledge of this place better than Buck does."

I stopped near a magnolia tree that had seen generations of family life on this farm. "Sam, can you cut a few of those small lower branches?"

As he leaned over to snip some of the green-ery I said, "There's a place I want to show you. We need to go today before the snow comes."

He looked at me, slightly amused. "Okay, want to tell me where?"

"Nope. You'll see."

"It is getting a little airish out here, you know," he teased.

We got back to the barn where Buck was finishing his chores. "Buck, we need to use the farm truck. Is that okay? I would take the horses, but I'm a little afraid of the weather."

"Sure," he said. "You know where it is."

I found the 1978 blue and white farm truck in the shed off the back of the barn. Sam got in, and I climbed up on the bench seat beside him.

Its smell instantly took me back to riding with Daddy to check cows. It had smell all its own—a combination of diesel fuel fumes com-ing from the cans in the back mixed with the aroma of sweetness of cow or horse feed, and the metallic smell of rust from tools pushed underneath the bench seat. Gray tape made a stripe down the middle of that seat as it tried to hold the seat cover together. Buck must use the truck on a pretty regular basis because it cranked on the first try.

"Where are we going?"

"Just head out, and I'll tell you."

Sam was able to see a faint trace of a path that led from the barn down a hill to a deeper part of the woods. We had only gone a short distance when I told him to stop. I got out first and held out my hand for him to follow. Walking into a clearing, I pointed up the next embankment.

Taking his hand, I led him to the foot of the tallest tree in sight, an American Beech, my name tree. I just looked at his face as he knelt and traced the signatures with his long fingers.

"Recognize any?"

"Well, I see new carvings that must be Buck and Simsie's, and I see your name. How old were you when you did this?"

"About twelve I guess. See, there is Asa's name and my mother's—Beth, my granddaddy and grandmother. There are Buck's initials. He did that not long before I did mine as a kid. There are many, but as the tree ages, the signatures don't climb up the tree with growth, they just widen at the same level and eventually are unreadable. Look, there is another 'V.' I don't remember it being there before."

Another initial. What in the world could this mean? It was beginning to get a little creepy.

Sam was taking it all in—the tree and the mamrkings. Since he is a carver, I could tell he liked it.

"Only family names here?" he asked still walking around the base of the tree.

"Mostly. I think an occasional hunter must have carved on it when they were here. That's okay with me."

Walking around the tree with Sam, I wrapped my arms around his waist and looked up at him. "You want to sign my tree?"

His eyes widened. I couldn't tell if he was surprised or ready to bolt and run. He pushed my hair back from my face and kissed me lightly.

"I'd be honored."

Like Daddy, he took out his pocket knife and carefully made the outline of a heart. He carved the background in relief so the initials would stand out instead of being carved into the tree. It had taken Sam almost an hour to do the carving. Our fingers were freezing and turning purple. The heart containing our initials was the most beautiful carving on the tree.

"Are we taking a step forward?" he asked.

"There's something I haven't told you," I said looking up at him as he gave me a concerned look. "My grant project fell through. I got a letter a few weeks ago telling me that the funding has been discontinued."

"So.....what are you going to do? Does this mean you're not going back to West Virginia?"

"I don't know if we are stepping into Mississippi or back to West Virginia," I said. "I just want to be with you wherever we go. So for now, I still have unfinished business in the mountains."

Sam smiled down on me with a look of relief in his face. We got back in the truck and rode back to the house in a comfortable silence.

Chapter 27
Lora • 1998 • Mississippi

I woke up this morning feeling about as nervous as I imagine a bride should be. Daddy would be so happy to see Buck taking this huge life step. Simsie had already found a place in Asa's heart, from what I'm told.

After helping with a few last minute details, Sam and I came back to the house to get ready. There has still been no word from Paulette as to whether she is coming or not. I can see the uncertainty wearing on Buck. One minute he is smiling, the next he is brooding. Simsie, on the other hand, is radiant.

As I put on my dress, I was proud of how it

looked and fit. Just right for a country wedding. Sam must have thought so too by the look in his eyes. He looked great in starched khakis, sports coat and new boots.

We drove through the silent woods to the little church. There was a slight dusting of snow. With candles burning in the windows on this snowy evening, the church looked magical. Snow in our part of Mississippi is not too common. So this little snow seemed like a special blessing for the wedding. Just enough to be pretty but not enough to impede travel. This little snow shower is nothing compared to the snow in West Virginia.

We waited at the back of the church to be seated. I was to be seated in place of the mother of the groom in case Paulette didn't come.

Looking around the small crowd, my eyes froze when I saw her. It had been years since I'd seen her, but I knew her immediately. Her long hair was now cut shorter into a more fashionable style with just a hint of gray at her temples. A young woman, I guessed her daughter, was at her side.

I couldn't help but wonder if Buck had seen her.

"Paulette?" I said as I greeted her. She looked at me and smiled shyly. "I was certainly hoping you would come." I introduced her to Sam.

"Lora, you have grown up to be such a pretty woman," she said. "I'm still not sure I should be here. No telling how John really feels about me."

"I think he will be glad you are here," I reassured her.

"This is my daughter Randi," she said, looking over at her daughter.

"Hi, Randi. We are glad you are here, too. I think Buck will be thrilled to know he has a sister."

The girl didn't say much and looked down while I talked to her. She may not have known about Buck until all this came up. The pastor's wife came over to greet us and introductions were made. I was glad she had the task of serving as director for this small wedding. Sam and I excused ourselves, and the ladies talked about where Paulette should be in the wedding party.

Buck came out of one of the side rooms to greet us. "Lora, you sure do look pretty," he said, planting a kiss on my forehead. "You too,

Sam," he joked.

"I've never seen you look so good, Buck. Daddy would be amazed at you, all dressed up." I hesitated. "Buck, your mama and sister are here," I told him as I watched him scanning the room. They are over there getting instructions from Mrs. Simpson. Immediately, I could see a worried look come over his face.

"It's okay. Go over there and see her and meet your sister. Your mama is about as nervous as you are. Go on."

I watched the awkward reunion from across the church. It was time for us to sit down, so Sam and I took our place, on the groom's side. That really just included Shelly, his sister Randi, and us.

Listening to the quiet piano music, I bowed my head, asking God for special blessings that day. I hadn't noticed the wedding program until then. It was beautifully printed on cream paper. Simsie had done them herself, and they were just perfect.

*Join us today in celebrating the union
of John Vincent Toliver
and*

*Mary Simmons Montgomery
This 28th day of February, 1998
Crossroads Church
Crossroads, Mississippi*

The words on the paper seemed to jump out at me. I never knew Buck's middle name was Vincent. Could he be named for my daddy? That would explain a lot. My feelings and emotions were running wild. So many hints that I had ignored over the years suddenly boiled to the surface.

Could Buck be my brother? Why didn't Daddy tell me, or Buck for that matter? Did my mother know about him? Why had I never realized his gray-blue eyes looked just like Asa's?

The rest of the wedding was a blur. I could

tell Sam knew something was wrong. He kept reaching for my hand and squeezing it. Somehow I made it through the service.

As soon as it was over, I headed outside as quickly as I could. Maybe walking in the cold evening air would clear my head, so I could go back in and not ruin the special night. Small solar lanterns provided a little light along the paths. Wandering over to the little cemetery beside the church, I stood looking down at Asa's grave.

Asa Vincent Sinclair

I felt a slight tap on my shoulder. Turning, I saw Paulette standing there, giving me a sad and knowing look.

"Why didn't I know Buck was my brother?" I asked, tears finally stinging my eyes. "I'm not upset that he is. I just want to know why, why nobody told me."

She reached out and took my hand. "Lora, I thought you might have figured it out by now. Don't think bad of your daddy. This happened before your mama came along. It's a long story. A story for another day. Let's go back in."

"Does Buck know?"

"Pretty sure he does, but I've never told him.

He wants to belong so bad." She took my hand as we walked away from Asa's grave, along the path and back to the glowing little country church. We didn't say a word.

Back in the church, guests were congratulating the couple. Simsie was stunning with her long auburn hair falling past her shoulders. Buck was all smiles. Sam looked at me with questioning eyes.

I squeezed his hand. "I'm okay," I said. "We can talk later." Going through the motions of the reception, I began to relax.

When the reception was over, I was clearing tables, washing punch cups and helping in any way I could. Buck came over to give me a goodbye hug.

"Thank you Lora for all you have done. Not just tonight, but always."

"You are welcome, my brother." Buck looked at me with surprise in his eyes. "Buck, did you know you were my brother? I never figured it out until I saw your middle name on the program."

He swallowed and stared at me for a second or two. "I felt like I was, but I never knew for sure. How did......," he was at a loss for words.

"We will talk when you get back. You and Simsie have a great getaway."

He hugged me again. "Oh, I always hoped for this!"

He turned and rushed to meet his bride, but hesitated and turned back to give me one more smile. I can't wait to hear Paulette's story.

ACKNOWLEDGEMENTS

As a person who has had a 37-year career as a journalist, I found it difficult to write fiction. I'm used to "just the facts, ma'am" type of writing. When I returned to college more than ten years ago, I told one of my professors from The University of Mississippi that I was afraid to write fiction, especially dialogue. He advised me to keep reading good fictionand studying the dialogue. I did—too many good authors to name.

The setting for *The Carving Place* is a real place—or it was. Sinclair Farm was inspired by the home of my grandparents, Cathey S. and Ollie May Dupuy Dandridge in Barr, Miss.

The house described here was real. Built in 1856, it burned in 1981. It exists today in my memories and in those of my cousins. The name tree still stands tall in the woods behind my house.

The characters are entirely fictitious. Asa has some of the characteristics of my daddy, Hayley Cathey Dandridge, to whom the book is dedicated, but his character and life events are entirely fictitious.

I turned to my friend Tom McLaughlin, a native of West Virginia, for his input on the traditions, culture and dialects of West Virginia. Online help came from wvculture.org.

A personal interview with dulcimer maker Warren A. May of Berea, Ky., gave me details on dulcimer making. May has made more than 17,000 dulcimers from his Kentucky shop.

Information on the lives of West Virginia coal miners came from dhhr.wv.gov.

Most of the information on Mississippi culture and dialects comes from observation, being a native of this beautiful state for sixty-two years.

Thanks to Patricia Neely-Dorsey for allowing me to use her poem *Ancestors* in the forward. Northwest Mississippi Community College literature instructor Beth Leishman Adams was kind enough to be the first proofreader.

Oxford, Miss. best-selling author Julie Cantrell provided constructive criticism on plot structure and character development. My horse trainer friend and author Michelle Tomars Kuester coached me on continuity in the written word just as she reminds me of continuity in the saddle.

Much gratitude goes to The Honorable Melvin McClure Jr., friend, author, attorney, and retired judge, for his inspiration, guidance, and help in getting this project off the ground.

What would I do without my friend Tammy Gallina? She produced artwork on demand and put up with myspur-of-the-moment demands. Her acrylic painting of the real carving tree for the cover is perfect.

I'm so glad to have a found a local outlet in Laurel Rose Publishing. Thanks Chad Martin for answering my many questions. Heartfelt-thanks go to friends and family, especially my husband Howard, who believed I could write something besides news.

ABOUT THE AUTHOR

Nancy Dandridge Patterson had a 37-year career in broadcasting, journalism, and public relations. Her career began in small market radio in Mississippi. As manager of Northwest Mississippi Community College's National Public Radio Station, she was the youngest manager, at 23, in the nation-wide system.

She transferred to the college's Public Relations Department in 1988 where she won numerous state and regional awards in feature writing, sports writing, advertising, and photography.

Since retiring in 2010, Patterson has written for several local and regional magazines including *DeSoto Magazine* and *Hills and Harvest*, and also for newspaper publications. She fulfilled her first retirement goal of learning to quilt and has been prolific as a free-style, folk-type quilter.

A lifelong equestrienne, Patterson recently resumed riding after a 13-year break. Instead of showing with her daughters on the Quarter Horse circuit, she now trail rides with a special group of friends.

She resides on family farmland with her husband, Howard, her horses, two silky terriers, a black Labrador, and a Border Collie rescue dog. The Pattersons are the parents of three grown children, and have four grandchildren.

Read an excerpt from the second installment in this series of novellas from Nancy D. Patterson.

Chapter 1
Paulette • 1968 • Mississippi
The Bargain

I was never able to attend school for more than a year in one place. My parents are flea market people. They went from one flea market to another. We made stops at farmer's markets, tent sales, and anywhere we could set up as vendors. Daddy drove an old truck with a ratty camper that fit in the bed of the truck

Mama and I shared a bed in the camper, over the top of the cab. Daddy slept on the couch. We also had to carry all our stuff— some glassware, small furniture pieces if they will fit in the truck, but our specialty is books. Not just old junky paperback books, but the kind you would find in a rich person's wood-paneled library. People buy books because they like the author or the subject, but they also buy them because they are pretty.

So mama and I went to estate sales and looked for pretty leather-bound books or new books that still had the jackets in good condition. Some people just like to decorate with them. I guess it makes them look smarter than they are.

Our books are so nice you really wouldn't expect to find them at a flea market. But we also had some smalls—little odds and ends that don't cost much. We just don't have room for much more. We keep the books in a metal footlocker in the camper under the sofa.

Most kids at school didn't know how I live, but they know it's not a life like When I was a teenager, I started packing a little bag and freshen up in the school bathroom early before the bell rang. I knew one of the girls was bound to catch me one day, and then she will tell. I can't think of another single soul who comes to school early in the morning smelling of corndogs and cotton candy.

I buy most of my clothes at the flea markets. Sometime I get lucky and find something really cute at one of the other booths. Once I got a brand new pair of shoes. That booth had discontinued but new shoes. I try hard to fit in at school.

The year Daddy discovered that there were bunches of flea markets and farmer's markets in north Mississippi, he told us we were going there and stay the whole school year.

Turns out I stayed much longer.

LAUREL ROSE PUBLISHING

Laurel Rose Publishing is a small publishing company located in North Mississippi. The company was created as a way for unknown authors to get published and get help in marketing their works. If you are interested in publishing a book and want to know how you can do so, contact us at www.laurelrosepublishing.com.

INSPIRATIONS

The Cathey Place

This old farmhouse served as headquarters for several generations of Hayleys, Catheys, and Dandridges. Built in 1856 as a dogtrot cabin, it burned in 1981.

It had two original pens seperated by a dogtrot open hall. It underwent many add-on rooms and changes over the years, but the original rooms remained intact.

I was fortunate to spend most weekends and every Sunday at the farm with my daddy, grandmother and granddaddy.

Cash in Black

As noted previously, these characters were inspired by a composite of people you might meet in this area of the South during the time periods noted.

There is one exception. Providing comic relief in a book that is sometimes serious is Goose, the black lab. He is based on my own dog, Jake's Cash in Black.

Jilly

Providing inspiration for Sister is my Border Collie rescue dog Jilly. We found Jilly at the Senatobia-Tate County Animal Shelter in 2010. She is a graduate of beginning obedience training. Jilly has been a blessing from day one.

The Corncrib

The corncrib is one of the few remaining outbuildings that remains on the property of my ancestors, now owned by my cousins. I took this photo several years to showcase the quilt for a photo exhibition of quilts for a local club. The quilt is the 1939 friendship quilt described in the book.

CPSIA information can be obtained
at www.ICGtesting.com
Printed in the USA
FFOW01n0738040418
46150180-47312FF